Whispering Springs

Jerri Garretson

Ravenstone Press
Manhattan, Kansas
2002

Copyright © 2002 by Geraldine A. Garretson

Ravenstone Press
P. O. Box 1791,
Manhattan KS 66505-1791
Tel: (785) 776-0556
raven@interkan.net

Publisher's Cataloging

Garretson, Jerri.
  The Secret of Whispering Springs / by Jerri Garretson
      p.   cm.
    Summary: When fourteen-year-old Cassie's family purchases an old stone mansion in the Flint Hills of Kansas, she finds herself dealing with a mysterious ghost and a desperate man.
ISBN 0-9659712-4-4 pbk.

[1. Ghosts -- Fiction. 2. Kansas -- Fiction. 3. Haunted Houses -- Fiction. 4. Mystery and detective stories.]   I. Title.

[Fic] 2002
Library of Congress Control Number: 2002100701

Printed at Manhattan, Kansas by Ag Press

In memory of the wonderful neighbors
who enriched my childhood,
especially

Miss Thirza Mossman

Tom and Dora Mason

and

Dr. O.W. Alm

-J.G.

The House on the Prairie

The house was awesome.

A stone mansion. Cassie never dreamed such a house existed way out here on a hidden Kansas ranch. Even with its windows and doors boarded up it looked magnificent. It belonged in the upscale section of some big city, not out here in the Flint Hills.

She stared from the car window. The late afternoon sun gave a warm glow to the stone, especially the tower room with the bay window. You could imagine a house like that with grand parties and deep secrets hidden in its walls, mysteries behind the weathered boards, maybe even a ghost in the tower. At least Ben would come up with that one.

"Well, what do you think?" her father asked.

"You're kidding, right, Dad?" she asked. "This can't be the house."

"Why not? You know I've always wanted an old stone house," he said. "Don't you like it?"

"Like it?" she said. "Of course I like it. I just don't believe it. What's it doing way out here?"

"A rancher named Gwynne built it in 1882. It's not the only stone house built on a ranch around here in the 1880s, just the grandest of them. No one has lived in it for almost five years, though, and nobody took care of it for a long time before that. It's going to be a lot of work to make it livable again."

"You're really buying it?" Cassie still couldn't quite believe it.

"Yes," her mother answered. "It's a steal. No one wants it, way out here with all that renovating needed, but we're getting it for next to nothing. Back taxes. It's a good thing, too, since we'll have to put a lot of money into it to fix it up."

"Let's go take a closer look," her dad said, getting out of the car.

Cassie jumped out of the car and ran up the stone steps to the porch. She peeked through a crack in the board covering what she supposed was one of the living room windows. It was so dark inside that she could see very little, but she could make out that the room wasn't empty. There were still old furnishings in there.

"Hey, Mom," she called. "Did you know they left furniture in here?"

"Yes, Cassie, we've been inside to look things over. Some of it is just worn out old junk we'll have to haul away, but there are some lovely antiques that may have been in the house since it was built. It will be fun to keep some of those pieces and imagine what the house was like all those years ago."

Cassie's little brother, Ben, had been absorbed in his electronic game and hadn't been paying much attention. Now he hopped out of the car and yelled, "Hey, Mom, there's a big old barn. Can I have a horse?"

"One thing at a time, Ben. We don't know anything about caring for horses, but who knows, once we live on a ranch." Mrs. Wade eyed the giant stone barn speculatively. "Of course, the barn would make a great art gallery and antique shop."

"Out here, Mom?" Cassie asked. "Who would come way out here to look for art and old furniture?"

"You might be surprised. If what you sell is good enough, people are willing to take a little drive."

"Little drive?" Cassie laughed. "Unless you live in Alma, it isn't a little drive, Mom." She pointed up the hill behind the house. "What's the small stone building, and what about that broken down shed?"

"The stone building is the spring house and I think the thing you call a shed is all that's left of the old homestead log cabin."

"You mean we'll have to get our water from the spring? No running water in the house? No way!"

Cassie's mother looked amused. "The spring water is good and there's an old pump out back, too. But don't worry, Cassie the house has regular faucets."

Ben ran to the old cabin and peeked in. "It's spooky in there," he yelled. "Lots of spider webs. Maybe snakes live in there, too. And ghosts."

"Don't go poking around in there. I don't know about ghosts, but snakes are a good bet. It's a long way to a hospital if you get bitten by a rattler or a copperhead."

"But Mom, maybe I'd just find a couple of ring-necks I can keep in a terrarium."

"Maybe, but it's not worth taking the chance. You can probably find ringnecks under rocks right here in the yard, once we have it mowed to a decent length. It looks like the prairie has taken over, doesn't it?"

"Can't we go inside?" Cassie asked.

"Until we get the boards off the windows, there isn't enough light to see much. The electricity isn't turned on. I don't think it would be safe for you to wander around in there now."

"But you can't bring us all the way out here and not even let us look inside," Cassie protested. "That's just not fair. We must have a flashlight in the car. I'll be careful. Dad, can't I have a look?"

"The house isn't officially ours yet."

"But you do have a key, don't you?" Cassie persisted. If she was going to live in this house, she wanted to see it NOW.

"I don't suppose it would hurt anything," her father said. "If you can find a working flashlight, I'll let you in through the back door. It's the only one not boarded up."

Cassie dug through the bag of tools in the trunk of the car and found a flashlight with a bright beam.

"I got it," she called, and headed for the back of the house. As she rounded the corner, she thought she caught a glimpse of someone quickly closing the back porch door. Must be my imagination, she thought.

Her dad followed her and unlocked the door. See? If someone had been there, it probably would have been unlocked. She didn't mention what she thought she saw. It didn't make any sense. She stepped inside the small enclosed porch and turned on the flashlight.

"Hey, wait for me," Ben called. He stampeded through the door. When he saw how dark it was, he stopped short. "It's spooky in here, too," he whispered. "Look at all the cobwebs and dust."

Cassie followed her brother, who cautiously shuffled his way through the boarded up porch leading to the kitchen. He opened the inner door. It creaked eerily in the beam of the flashlight and was quickly slammed shut from the inside. A piercing wail emanated from the kitchen.

Cassie and Ben turned and dashed through the porch door. They burst into the warm spring sunshine and ran for the car.

"Cassie! Ben! What's the matter?" their mother asked.

"It's haunted!" Ben shouted. "There's something awful in there. It slammed the door on me and screamed."

Dad gave Cassie a questioning look. They all knew Ben had a big imagination. It wasn't surprising he was spooked by a dark, dusty old house.

"It's true, Dad," said Cassie. "Just like he said. There's something weird in that house."

"You're sure about this?" he asked. "Mom and I didn't see anything odd when we were in there. Probably plenty of mice we'll have to get rid of."

"Well, there's something in there now!" Cassie said firmly.

"It's probably just an animal that got in somehow. A cat, maybe. Cats can yowl pretty nasty. I'll take a look," he said, taking the flashlight from Cassie.

"Yeah, but cats don't slam doors," Ben pointed out.

"If there is someone in there, it might not be safe to go snooping around. It could be a fugitive that broke in. Shouldn't we call the police?" asked her mother.

"The door probably just swung shut, or maybe there's a draft in there from a broken window somewhere," Dad said. "Come on, Karen. You know your way around in there better than I do." They headed back to the door.

Cassie and Ben lagged behind at first but then they trailed along to watch.

"Wait here," their dad said. "He pulled open the door to the back porch and checked to be sure no one was there. "The coast is clear so far," he said. He took a few steps to the inner door and turned the knob. It was locked. Surprised, he turned back to look at his wife.

"The kids didn't lock this door, and it wasn't locked before," he said. "Maybe it locked when it blew shut. I think the same key opens this lock, too."

The key worked and he slowly pushed open the door. It sounded like a long groan. Before stepping inside he beamed the flashlight around the kitchen. "Nothing unusual in there from what I can see," he said. He stepped in and their mom followed. Cassie and Ben waited outside.

"I hope the werewolf doesn't get them," Ben said.

"There's no such thing as werewolves," Cassie said. "There's no werewolf in there."

"It sounded like a werewolf to me," Ben insisted.

"So when did you ever hear a werewolf?" Cassie challenged him. "Just in some movie, right? Like that's real."

"So what do you think it was, if it wasn't a werewolf?" Ben asked.

"Maybe dad's right. It's probably just a cat," Cassie replied. She was tired of staring at the back door, waiting for her parents. "Let's go look in the barn."

The Barn

Ben trotted after her. He was always ready for some new distraction.

The barn wasn't boarded up like the house but the big sliding door was either too heavy for Cassie to open or it was fastened in some way. On the uphill side she saw a ramp that led to a smaller door and headed for that. Ben dashed ahead of her and pushed the door open just enough to squeeze inside. He bolted back out quickly.

"I'm not going in there," he said. "It's dark and scary, too. Maybe the whole place is full of were-wolves and ghosts."

"Oh, Ben," said Cassie, "Why would ghosts and werewolves want to live in an old barn?" She peered into the gloom and edged through the narrow open-ing. "This place is huge, Ben. We could have a whole herd of horses if we wanted to." She was surprised to see light coming in at the far end. She walked toward it, and as she neared the end stall, she felt a light, cold breeze that seemed to swirl around her. The farther she got, the stronger it was, as though it were trying to wrap itself around her.

Cassie whirled around. Where was it coming from? She felt goose bumps on her arms and her ears prickled from soft whispery sounds in the strange breeze. She hadn't noticed any wind outside. The strange breeze continued to press around her. She had the oddest feeling it was urging her toward the stall at the end. She looked in and stepped back in surprise. Someone was living there.

She could make out a bedroll in the hay, a pack filled with some kind of supplies, a small table and chair, and a camp stove. Hanging on a hook were a faded dirty jean jacket, a pair of patched old pants and a coiled rope. In a cardboard box were a few groceries. She didn't see anyone around.

The whispering sounds grew more insistent. Cassie had an unmistakable feeling that something was warning her. What if whoever was living in the barn was in the house right now? What if her parents were in danger? She ran to the door, squeezed through it, and dashed for the house.

"Ben," she called over her shoulder. "Stay out of there. It's not safe." She didn't know how she knew it wasn't safe, but she knew. Whoever lived in that barn was not going to be a friend.

"Mom, Dad!" she yelled into the back door. "Get out of there quick!"

Her parents were in the kitchen, just ready to leave the house. "What's the matter, Cassie?" her mother asked.

"There's someone living in the barn," she said,

13

pointing. "And he's not in there now, so he might be in the house or somewhere else around here."

"Surely not," her dad said. "We didn't find anything in the house. What's this about the barn? You kids certainly are full of imagination today. I hope you aren't going to be like this once we move in."

"Dad, it's not my imagination," Cassie insisted. She told him exactly what she had seen. "I don't think he's friendly. Let's leave now."

"Cassie, this is going to be our home. If there's a problem with some squatter who has moved into the barn, we'll take care of it. The place has been deserted for years. Perhaps someone who doesn't have a home thought the old barn would be a safe place to spend some time." He started for the barn with Cassie following him.

"Dad, don't go in there," Cassie pleaded. "Let's go home. She looked toward the house to see if her mother would stop him, and gasped. A board on one of the windows of the third story tower room had been removed and a man with a beard was watching them.

"Look, Dad," she whispered, grabbing his arm and pointing to the window, but by the time he looked, the face was gone.

"Cassie, what's wrong? Now you really do look like you've seen a ghost," her mother said.

Cassie described the face she saw at the window. Nothing was there now, just the dark window pane. "He was there, watching us," she said. "Maybe it's the man who's living in the barn."

Her mother raised an eyebrow questioningly and put an arm around her. It was Ben that had the runaway imagination, not Cassie. "Daniel, are you sure we checked everywhere in the house?" she asked.

"Everything but the attic," he said. "Do you think there actually was someone in the house?"

"Cassie saw him, and if she's found evidence of someone living in the barn, it's possible," she said. "If he is in the house, he can't be in the barn right now. Let's have a look and leave him a note about finding another place to live. If he's still around next time we come, we'll call the sheriff." She rummaged around in her purse for a notepad and pen, wrote a note and handed it to her husband. "What do you think?" she asked.

Cassie peered at the note in his hand and read it aloud. "'This property has been abandoned for several years, but it is now being purchased by a family. Please vacate the premises immediately. If you have questions, please contact Daniel or Karen Wade at 785 - . . .'" She paused, surprised. "Mom, are you sure you want to give this person our home phone number?" she asked.

"Who else would he call?"

"I don't know, but I don't want to hear from him," Cassie said.

"We probably won't. Most likely, he'll just clear out and look for another place to camp. If he gives us any trouble, I'm sure the sheriff can handle it. Since you're worried, I'll just give him my cell phone number." She took the note back and changed the number. "Come on, Cassie, show me where his things are in the barn and I'll pin the note on something." She started for the barn.

"You won't hear from him on any telephone," said Ben. "He's probably a ghost. You'll hear from him at night when he makes scary sounds, like that sound we heard in the house before."

Cassie rolled her eyes. That was no ghost she had seen in the window. And no ghost would need a bedroll and groceries. "I'm coming, Mom," she said.

As Cassie slipped into the barn with her mother, she felt the cold breeze again. She thought she could hear someone or something breathing, right next to her ear. The whispering started again. Her goose bumps came back and she began to shiver.

Her mother didn't seem to feel anything unusual. She used an old paperclip she found in her purse to fasten the note to the jean jacket and they left the barn.

"Daniel," she said. "Cassie's right. It certainly looks as though someone has been camping out in that barn. I hope he moves on and doesn't give us any trouble. Let's go home. Next time we come, the papers will be signed and we can actually get to work on this place. It will be ours."

Jordan

on't tell me your dad actually bought that haunted house out on Mill Creek. It's probably dangerous. My grandmother says nobody's even lived in it for years." Jordan looked horrified. "How can you even think of moving out there? It's so far away. When will we ever see each other?"

Cassie didn't know what to say. She wasn't exactly thrilled about that either. She would miss living right next door to Jordan, her best friend for the past three years. Even though the old house was gorgeous, she kept remembering the face at the window, finding out someone was living in the barn, and having the kitchen door slammed in her face by something horrible. She rubbed her arms as she remembered the strange cold that enveloped her in the barn. Did that really happen?

She had to admit she was tired of the cramped house she lived in now. There were so many rooms in the prairie house she thought she might ask for two rooms all for herself, one for a bedroom, the other for an art studio. That sounded wonderful, even if the beautiful old place was a shambles. Her parents had convinced her that the tramp, if that's what he was, would be gone. And there was so much space out on the prairie. You could see forever from the hilltops.

Jordan babbled on, "You'll probably go nuts from the wind and loneliness, like those pioneer women who couldn't stand it. And if the place really is haunted, who knows what kind of awful things might happen? I bet there's a reason that house has been empty for years."

"We're going to fix it up, you know," Cassie said. "It's not like we're just going to move into a house with no hot water or anything. Besides, why would it be haunted?"

"Who knows what kind of stuff happened out there? Something must have scared people off. People don't just abandon houses for no reason."

"Dad says the last guy who lived there died several years ago and for awhile no one knew where any of his family was. They finally found his daughter living in Minnesota but no one in the family wanted the old place. Finally the county took it over to sell for back taxes. It's a bargain."

"Some bargain," Jordan said. "You'll spend so much making the place livable, you won't have anything left. I mean, does it even have doors or just boards nailed to the frame? Who knows if the floors are even safe to walk on?"

"Of course the floors are safe! My parents have been all through the house and inspected it. My dad's an architect and he wouldn't buy a place that isn't structurally sound," Cassie said. "How do you know so much about it, anyway?"

"Kevin's been out there a few times. He told me about it. He goes hunting on that land. He and his buddies explored it. He even brought home an old horseshoe he found out there last time. Said he hoped it would bring him good luck not bad, since the old place gave him the creeps. One place, the dogs wouldn't even go. They just stopped in their tracks, didn't even bark, just stopped. He had to take them another way. They even found a couple of old graves."

"Graves?" Cassie asked, surprised. "Why would there be graves out there?"

Jordan tried a new approach. "Haven't you and your family even explored the whole property? Want to go camping out there with me, before your parents start fixing the place up? Maybe we can roll out our sleeping bags right by the graves. That ought to be the best place to find ghosts. If we do it before you move, we can even write it up for the school newspaper. 'Cassie Wade and Jordan Dexter, Ghostbusters Extraordinaire.'"

Cassie pursed her lips and sighed. "Sure, Jordan. Like our parents are going to let two fourteen-year-old girls camp out there alone. As if you even had the nerve."

Jordan pulled on a ragged sweatshirt and stuffed her feet into her sneakers. "You better find out all you

19

can before you move out there, that's all. Don't think I'm going to come spend a weekend with you if the place is crawling with ghosts howling all night long. I'm having Sunday dinner at my grandmother's house. I'll ask her what the old stories say."

"Fine, you just do that. Be sure you don't leave out a single detail when you call me to tell me how awful my new home is going to be," Cassie retorted, pretending to be huffy. Secretly, she didn't know whether she felt more scared, excited, or disbelieving.

Rumors

Maybe Kevin would take her out there to look around without her parents, thought Cassie. He had his own pickup truck. He could tell her all about what he'd found when he was hunting on Old Man Cranston's land. But Kevin wasn't just hanging around waiting for his kid sister's best friend to ask him a favor like that, and anyway, Jordan would have insisted on going along.

Ordinarily, she would have been delighted to have Jordan with her anywhere, but she wasn't ready to admit that Jordan's ghost story hype had actually gotten her interested. Maybe Ben was right after all, and the place really was haunted.

No, she'd have to rely on Mom and Dad, which shouldn't be too hard. Now that the "prairie property," as Dad called it, was officially theirs, they'd be going out there every chance they got to work on the repairs. As far as she could tell, if they tried to do it all themselves they wouldn't be moving out there for another five years. The trick was going to be finding a way to do something *besides* work on the house.

Cassie didn't come up with a good plan in the short distance between Jordan's house and hers. "Hi, Mom, I'm home," she shouted as she came in the back door. She dropped her backpack on the kitchen floor and headed for the refrigerator. Jordan always offered her soda and snacks, but Cassie preferred milk with heaps of Carnation Chocolate Malted Mix in it.

Cassie's mother appeared in the kitchen doorway wearing faded and paint-splattered jeans and a sweatshirt, her hair tied up under an old bandanna. There were bits of leaves clinging to her clothes and hair. "Hi, yourself," she said. "Make one for me, too?"

As she mixed a second chocolate malt for her mother, Cassie debated with herself. Should she just come right out and tell her mother she wanted to explore their new home for graves and ghosts?

"Did you walk home with Jordan?" her mother asked.

"Yeah, and she tried to scare me out of moving out to the prairie," Cassie answered. "Some big story about ghosts haunting the place and graves out there. I guess Ben isn't the only one who thinks it's spooky. And after what I saw the other day, I'm wondering, too."

"I wouldn't worry much about it. People always seem to have stories about run-down old houses, just like that old derelict place down the street. We've never seen anything ghostly there, though. I think people just get a kick out of making up stories. Aren't old houses supposed to be spooky, just for the fun of it? Our house won't look remotely spooky when we get done fixing it up. We asked the sheriff to check the barn to see if the man is gone before we spend a lot of time out there."

Her mother paused and looked reflective for a moment. "But there were some stories about the place years ago. I haven't heard any more about them since I was a kid, and even then, they were just silly rumors."

"What kind of rumors?" Cassie asked.

"Out there in the hills, they said, there was a place where you could hear whispering, but no one was there. On nights when the moon was full, there was a strange mist that floated over the place and there were whispers all around the house. No one I knew ever heard any whispering -- just coyotes howling at night. And the mist, if there ever was one, was most likely just fog.

"There were some high school kids who got Old Man Cranston's permission to spend a weekend out there camping when I was in about fifth grade. They came back telling all kinds of wild tales. Later, they admitted they made it all up and nothing unusual happened at all, except that Joe Becker went wandering around in the night and fell in the creek and Alan Johnson nearly pitched the tent on top of an ant hill.

"I was out there today trying to clear enough

brush to make a decent pathway to the house so we can really get to work. Didn't see anything spooky at all. First thing we've got to do is pull those boards off the doors and put in new locks so we can get in and out of the house properly. Then we'll get some contractors to take a look at the plumbing and wiring. I can handle cleaning, painting and wallpapering, but I'm not messing with that code stuff. Good thing we have your dad."

"You mean, we don't know whether the wiring is safe?" Cassie could hardly believe it. "You never told me that. Jordan said the place is in such bad shape it's probably dangerous. Jordan says we'll probably crash right through the floors to the basement. Maybe we'll all die in a fire."

"Oh, Cassie, don't be silly. The place is overgrown and some of the window panes were shot out by punks with air rifles before they were boarded up but the roof is sound and the floors are fine. The wiring isn't that old, though. I think Cranston had it put in around 1950. There's nothing wrong with it, but it isn't ready for modern demands. We'll need to rewire it before we move in."

"Can I have my own art studio?" Cassie asked. "With track lighting?" Was it too much to hope for? "How long is all this going to take, before we actually move out there, I mean?"

"Dad and I think by midsummer we can move in. Of course, there will still be a lot of work to do, but the place is big enough that if we get the cleaning, wiring and plumbing done, and a phone put in, we can sort of 'camp out' in a few rooms while we work on the rest." She smiled. "Your own art studio? I'm sure you'd enjoy that. Track lighting isn't a bad idea. If we plan all the wiring and fixtures at once, it will save us time and expense later. I'll talk it over with Dad."

"Thanks, Mom!" Cassie said. She finished her malted milk and hoisted her backpack. "And Mom," she said as she headed for her room, trying to make it look like a casual afterthought, "Can Jordan and I have a campout there some weekend soon?"

"Two girls alone way out there? Not on your life," her mother answered. "But after we move in, if you want to camp out on the prairie near enough to the house that I think it's safe, you can try it."

Miss Mossman

No matter what was out there on the prairie a bigger room would have to be an improvement. Cassie barely had space to walk between her desk and bed. Her collection of fossils and semiprecious stones was stuffed in boxes on the floor and under the desk. Her art supplies were in more boxes on top of those and stacked on a closet shelf. Her books wouldn't even fit into the overflowing bookcase. There wasn't much room to hang any of her paintings, either, and the only space to paint was on the small desk. When they moved in three years ago, Dad said this place was only temporary, while they saved enough for a down payment on a big house with a large piece of land. To Cassie, it felt like eternity.

She chucked her backpack onto the chair, kicked off her shoes and flopped on the bed. Somehow, she always thought that when they moved, it would be to some nice, new house Dad would build in town, even though Dad always talked about owning an old house and land and living out on the prairie.

She liked hiking on the prairie, but would she like living there? With ghosts?

What kind of ghosts would be way out there? Some cranky old gunslinger looking to even the score? One of those lonely pioneer women Jordan teased her about, who pined away for neighbors and a city life, moaning and sighing in the wind? An Indian? Funny, she'd never heard of anyone being haunted by an Indian. Why not? Were ghosts the same no matter what language they spoke or what culture they came from? Cassie imagined a tall Sioux warrior with a magnificent war bonnet and beaded shirt, partly transparent, a wisp on the wind. Could she paint that?

Cassie was getting out her sketchbook and drawing pencils when Ben came stomping up the stairs, making all the noise he could, and rattled her doorknob. Couldn't he ever just go past to his room without doing that? It was so much fun having a eight-year-old brother.

"Cassie," he called, "Can I borrow your sidewalk chalk?"

"What for?" she asked. "I don't want you to use it all up." It wasn't like she was saving it or anything, but Ben got carried away. He might decorate the sidewalk all the way down the block.

"It's Miss Mossman's birthday," said Ben. "I wanted to make a picture on her front walk."

Darn! How could she forget her neighbor's birthday? It wasn't like Mom hadn't reminded her a dozen times. She really loved Miss Mossman. After all, who taught her how to draw cats and play chopsticks on her piano?

Cassie pulled the bin of sidewalk chalk out from under the bed, yanked open the door and handed it to Ben. "When you get yours done, come get me so I can add something, too," she said.

Ben made a face.

"What's the matter with you?" she asked. "I gave you the chalk."

"Yeah, but the sidewalk drawing was MY idea. I don't want you adding anything to it," he protested. "It's not fair. You can draw better than me anyway. You'll just make mine look stupid."

"Okay, Ben," she said. "I'll make her some cookies and design a card for her. I think Mom's invited her over for dinner, too."

Ben grinned. "Thanks," he said. Off he went with the chalk.

Cassie looked at the sketchbook. The Indian drawing would have to wait. She'd have to get going on those cookies.

That evening, after they celebrated Miss Mossman's 90th birthday, she asked them about the house they were buying. Ben told her that were-wolves lived in it, and ghosts, and even snakes. She smiled and rumpled his hair. "Well, then, Ben, it should suit you and your imagination just fine," she said. "You and your imagination did a fine job of decorating my sidewalk, and Cassie's cookies are delicious." She helped herself to a third one.

"It's the old Cranston place," Cassie's mom told her. "It looks a bit neglected now, boarded up and all, but it's going to be beautiful."

"I had no idea the prairie place you talked about was the Cranston place," said Miss Mossman. "My mother had a photo of it. There was some kind of family connection. I never heard much about it, though. My mother lived in Nebraska all her life. As a kid, I always thought the house was in Nebraska. The picture was in a beautiful frame with a sealed envelope fastened to the back. It said, 'For Annie.' I never knew who Annie was.

"I didn't know where the house was until long after I moved here as a young woman to teach school. Then I heard rumors about the old place and many years ago when I saw a photo in the newspaper, I recognized it as the same house. By that time, my mother was dead and no one in the family could tell me anything about it. My grandmother might have had a sister who went to Kansas, but she died young. I don't think we had any Cranstons in our family."

"I'd love to see that old photo," said Cassie's dad. "It might help us in restoring the house, and if you cared to part with it, I'd like to hang it in the house."

"That's the odd thing, Daniel. I don't have it any more. I was going through my mother's trunk about a week ago and found it. Then it just disappeared. I had some men in doing repairs at my house around

29

that time. I thought one of them might have taken it, but why would they want an odd thing like that?"

"Did you ever look in the envelope?" asked Cassie. "It might tell you what the family connection was."

"No, I never had the chance. After my grandmother died, my mother packed the photo away in that trunk. I guess she thought none of us would be interested in it. After all, we didn't know whose or where it was. The trunk was left in the barn at our Nebraska farm after my mother died. When my brother died last fall the land was sold. My niece thought I might like to have Mother's trunk, but she didn't send it to me until just a couple of weeks ago.

"It took me awhile to go through it. When I found the photo in her things, I put it aside, planning to see what I could find out, but it disappeared before I got a chance to investigate. A few days ago I got a phone call from a man who didn't identify himself. He asked me a lot of questions about the Cranston place. I told him I didn't know a thing about it, but he didn't believe me. He told me he'd be in touch again and that I'd better cooperate. I have no idea what he meant by that. So far, he hasn't called back. And now you are buying the place. What an odd coincidence."

Cassie thought about the man in the barn. Maybe it wasn't some old bum passing through. Maybe he was at the Cranston place for a reason and wouldn't want to leave. Cassie shivered as she remembered the face at the tower window.

Whispering Springs

he house looked a lot less deserted when Cassie finally got a chance to go out there with her family again. There were no more boards on the windows and all the broken panes had been repaired. The front door was absolutely grand. It needed refinishing but it was decorated with exquisite scrollwork carvings and inset with beveled glass engraved with delicate iris patterns.

The yard no longer looked like part of the untamed prairie. Her dad said they had to hire someone with a tractor to come in and mow it, the grasses were so high. There was no more trace of someone camping in the barn.

It felt strange to walk right in the front door like it was their home, but it didn't feel like home at all. Cassie's mother had arranged to have the junk hauled away, swept the dust out and pushed the remaining furniture to one side in each room so they could really clean. Now, with sunlight streaming in the tall windows, the old rooms looked bright and inviting even without proper cleaning or real furnishings. The oak floors creaked when Cassie walked on them, but seemed solid enough.

This was her first chance to explore. She went through each room, looked out each window, checked in each closet. Cassie wished she could claim the room with the bay window on the second floor for her own, but she was sure her parents would want that one. She decided to ask for the two rooms on the west side. The back one had wonderful north light for an art studio, and the front one had a terrific view of the land.

When she opened the closet in the room she decided would be her bedroom, she found something scratched in the wood of the door post. It had been painted over so she could only make out part of it, "A---- G--nne, M-- 24, 18--." She traced the lines with a finger, trying to make out more letters, but they were too thickly covered with paint. Why would someone write on a door post? She looked out across the lawn and away across the rolling hills. In early spring, it was becoming lush and beautiful. The redbuds were in bloom.

Cassie suddenly felt dizzy, as if the room had shifted slightly. The air wavered as though it were thick. She put out a hand to steady herself and found she was holding a walnut four-poster bed that had not been there before. A cool breeze touched her cheek and arms, though the window wasn't open. It raised goose bumps on her arms and sent a shiver down her spine. Her heart thumped in her chest.

A soft voice whispered, "Can you see it like I saw it?

Cassie was aware that the house had changed around her. When she looked out the window, she saw that the lawn was different, too. There were fewer trees. Her parents' car wasn't parked on the gravel drive. A man she had never seen before was walking toward the barn, dressed in old-fashioned clothing.

The illusion only lasted an instant and then it was gone, leaving Cassie bewildered. Then fear set in. The cool breeze was much like the one she'd felt in the barn, but gentler. The house seemed full of uneasy secrets. She didn't believe in Ben's were-wolves, but something eerie was there. She ran down the stairs and out into the afternoon sun. Out there, what had just happened didn't seem possible. It couldn't have been her imagination, could it?

Her mother looked up from where she was painting the screen door frame. "Cassie, honey, what's the matter? You look like you've seen a ghost," she said.

"No, not a ghost," Cassie said, "but I just had some kind of vision of the past or something. It was a long time ago, and the house was all furnished. There was a man walking to the barn. You weren't here, and neither was our car. It only lasted a moment and I felt a cold breeze that gave me goose bumps."

"Oh, Cassie, don't let your imagination run away

with you just because it's an unfamiliar old house. I know it doesn't look homey or lived in yet. Maybe it was just an artistic inspiration. Don't you ever get them that way, like a flash of illusion, showing what you want to paint?"

"Not like this, Mom," Cassie replied. "And I know when something is from my own mind and when it's not."

"Your father and I haven't seen or heard anything unusual since we first looked at the place, except for the man who was camping out in the barn, but he's long gone. If the house were that strange, don't you think we would have seen something? We've spent hours working out here while you and Ben were in school. Nothing like that ever happened to us."

Cassie knew it would do no good to try to convince her mother. She was beginning to doubt it had happened herself. Maybe it *was* some kind of hallucination caused by hunger and thirst. She had skipped lunch at school that day, eager to keep working on her mosaic.

"Got anything to eat and drink out here?" she asked. Maybe a snack would help.

"I never come out here without a cooler," said her mother. "It's in the kitchen. Still no electricity, but we think the contractors are coming to finish the wiring next week."

Cassie headed for the kitchen. She called back to her mother, "Where's Ben?"

"He took a walk out to the upper spring. He's been there before with Dad, so we thought he could manage it by himself."

Ben, wandering around alone? They would never have allowed that in town, thought Cassie. They must feel really safe out here, even with the snakes. Ben thought he knew all about snakes, but she wasn't willing to bet on it.

In the kitchen, she helped herself to a bottle of water and found a ham sandwich and a banana. That's what I need, she thought. Food. And to get out of the house before I see another vision. She heard her dad working in the cellar. She hadn't been down there yet, and at the moment she had no desire to go. "Dad," she called down the stairs, "I'm going to find Ben and have him show me the spring. Tell Mom where I went."

She headed out the back door and up the hill on the path to the spring. It was a warm day. Wildflowers were beginning to bloom in the brush and the trees were starting to leaf out. She could hear a meadowlark singing. It all seemed so peaceful, but she still felt uneasy.

It was farther to the spring than she expected. By the time she got there, she had finished her lunch and tucked what was left of the bottle of water into her belt. Ben was playing in the mud and was half covered with it.

"Hi, Cassie," he said. "It's really cool. Water comes right up out of the ground and runs down the hill to the creek. Mom said they call the ranch 'Whispering Springs' and now I know why. If you listen, it sounds like someone is whispering, but you can't figure out what they are saying. I don't know if it's the water or the wind in the trees."

"Ben, you're a mess," Cassie said. "So this place has a name beside 'Old Man Cranston's Place.' I like 'Whispering Springs' a lot better."

"I never lived in a place with a name before," Ben said. "It seems special." He pointed. "There's an old cemetery over there."

So that's where it was. Jordan was right; there was a graveyard. But Jordan hadn't known about 'Whispering Springs.' That would surprise her.

"Did you go to the cemetery? Is it spooky?" she asked.

"No. There's just lots of weeds and a few grave stones. They're real old," he said. "Maybe that's where the ghosts come from. Listen, you can hear the whispering."

Whispering? Like she heard in the barn? She remembered the feeling of something warning her. Cassie kept quiet. At first she heard only the rustling of the tiny new leaves and the soft gurgle of the spring water, but the longer she listened, the more she was sure the whispering was something else. She could barely make it out, but it sounded like one word repeated over and over, "Beware. Beware."

Beware of what? Cassie spun around. Nothing seemed out of place or sinister. Who or what was warning her now? The whispering continued, "Beware, Beware."

"Ben, does the whispering sound like any words to you?" she asked.

"No, just soft noises," he answered. "Werewolves don't make sounds like that."

"Oh, Ben, you and your werewolves," she said. Why didn't he hear the words?

She started toward the little graveyard. At least she could tell Jordan who was buried there. Not far ahead she could see a white marble stone, weeds grown up tall around it. As she came closer, she suddenly glimpsed a man hustling away through the brush. She froze. Someone had been out here watching them. How long had he been watching Ben?

"Ben, I think it's time to head back to the house," she said, as steadily as she could. "Mom and Dad will be wondering about us by now."

He agreeably got up and followed her. As they started down the hill to the house, she kept hearing, "Beware, beware."

Beware of what? Beware of who? she wanted to shout, but she didn't want to scare Ben.

The Cellar

Back at the house, Cassie sat on the front porch hugging her knees. Should she tell her parents about the whispered warning and the person who had been skulking around?

Watching Ben, she thought. He was watching Ben, maybe watching all of us. What if she hadn't come along? What would the man have done? But so far, her parents hadn't believed anything she had told them about the strange occurrences around the place, except for the man living in the barn. At least there had been proof of that.

Was there any real danger, or was she imagining things? Why had she heard that voice whispering "beware"? The whole thing gave her the creeps.

Ben played in the yard, unconcerned. Why didn't he hear the voice, too? He dug a hole near the front porch with a stick, twisting it round and round.

"Look, Cassie," he shouted. "I found something. Here, it's for you." Ben dashed over to her, hand outstretched. On his palm was a dirty, tarnished piece of jewelry.

It was hard to tell what it was. Cassie picked it up gingerly. "Thanks, Ben. I'll see what it looks like cleaned up." Something to do. Something else to think about.

Cassie headed for the old pump near the back door. Amazing it still worked. She found a dented bucket and pumped it half full. She stuck the muddy lump into the water and rubbed it. It was so tarnished it was mostly black, even with the mud washed off, but now she could see that it was a graceful brooch shaped like a bouquet of irises. There was something engraved on the back, but she couldn't make it out. Where would something like that come from, way out here? She didn't think it belonged to Old Man Cranston.

Cassie slipped it into her pocket. "Thanks again, Ben. It's real pretty," she called, but Ben was off somewhere else now and didn't answer.

Her dad opened the back door. "Oh, there you are. I was wondering where you'd wandered off to. I could use some help carrying stuff up from the basement. There must be a train load of old junk down there."

"Anything interesting?"

"There might be but most of it looks like a lot of junk no one would want. Who knows? I just want to get it out of the basement so we'll have a place to keep the things we're using the fix up the house. Tools, paint, all that stuff. Something odd, though. I wouldn't have thought anyone would have been down there in years, but it looks like someone was rummaging through there searching for something."

"Do you think that man I saw in the house could have done it?" Cassie asked, careful to sound skeptical. She was sure that was the explanation, but she was equally sure Dad wasn't going for it.

"You're still sure you saw someone in the house, Cassie?" her dad asked. He gave her a quizzical look.

"Yes, Dad. And I still think he was the one who was living in the barn. I think he wants something."

Her dad laughed. "Well, then, I hope he found it and took it. One less thing for us to haul out of here. Who knows how many people investigated this place while it was vacant? That's why they finally had to board up the doors and windows, to keep people out. They would have destroyed the place."

"But Dad, what if he took something important?"

"I sure don't see what anyone could have found down there that would be important to us. If it was important to him, fine."

No use trying to get Dad to believe me, thought Cassie. She hoped there would be something fascinating in the stacks and bundles that littered the old cellar. If someone else thought there was, maybe it was still there and she would find it.

She followed him down the dark steps. Dad had fixed up a generator so they'd have some light down there or it would have been impossible to work, and scary, too. Everything was covered with dust and cobwebs.

By her sixth trip to the barn, she was distracted enough that the feeling of fear had diminished. The loads she carried out were mostly boxes of things like yellowed old newspapers, canning jars and musty old clothes. She wondered if she could clean up the clothes and get anything for them at a vintage clothing store.

Now that she was calmed down, she knew for sure she needed to tell her father about the man she saw by the graveyard. "There was a man up there near the graveyard this afternoon. I think he was watching Ben. He sneaked off when I saw him. Maybe it was the same man who was living in the barn."

"You think you actually saw someone again, Cassie?" her father asked. He looked at her with a slight frown. He seemed unconvinced.

"Yes, I saw him," she said. "It's not my imagination. That's why I told Ben we had to come back to the house. But I didn't tell him about the man. I didn't want to scare him."

"I'll check around out there to see if there is any sign of someone hiding out or trampling the grass. I doubt that we have anything to worry about. If there was someone, it probably was a hunter who left when he saw you two kids there. Adam Cranston allowed hunters on his land and they've been coming out here for years."

Cassie didn't argue with her dad. How could she persuade him that the man was dangerous? She decided to try another question. "Did you know this place was called Whispering Springs?"

"Sure. Romantic name, isn't it? I think I'll put it on a sign where you turn onto our drive from the main road."

"But how did it get that name?" She hoped her dad could explain it better than her mom had.

"I don't know if anyone can say for sure, but there are old stories about people hearing a voice near the springs and around the house. Supposedly, it sounded like a girl or a young woman whispering but no one could ever make out what she said."

"I heard it today, Dad. At first I couldn't make it out, either, but then, just before I saw the man sneaking off, it sounded like, 'Beware, beware.'"

"Oh, Cassie! Ben sees werewolves around every tree and bush. Those I'm willing to pass off as his grandiose imagination, but you've never been one to come up with stuff like that. Ever since the first day we brought you out here you've been having visions or hallucinations or something. This has got to stop."

"Dad, they aren't visions. I really saw them. I heard the voice." How could she make him believe her? "The man in the barn was real. Maybe he didn't leave. Maybe he just moved out of the barn and is hanging out somewhere else nearby."

Dad raised his eyebrows. "I told you I'd take a look. Meanwhile, don't let YOUR imagination run away with you. You're fourteen, after all. It's one thing when you're eight like Ben." He hoisted another load and started up the stairs. "You'll feel better when things are homier around here."

So he didn't believe her, not that she thought he would. She squared her shoulders. No sense even talking with her parents about it. She hoped she could handle it on her own.

She looked around for another load to haul out to the barn. There was a treadle sewing machine in the corner. It was too heavy for her to carry but on top of it she found some old tin boxes. The patterns on them were faded and scratched but still pretty. Maybe we could sell them on the internet, she thought. Someone probably collects them. Or maybe Mom really would open an antique shop in the barn.

She brushed the dust off one of the tins and opened it. To her surprise, it was full of old letters, bundles of them tied in fragile satin ribbons. The handwriting was fancy and old-fashioned. She touched them softly. As soon as she did so, a cold invisible hand closed over hers and held it for a moment. She heard the whispering again. This time it said, "Read them."

Cassie looked around. No one was there. Her dad was still out in the barn.

"Who are you?" Cassie asked, trembling. "Why am I the only one who can hear you?"

There was no reply.

A Letter From the Past

Cassie shivered, her feet rooted to the cellar floor, her heart beating fast. After a few moments, she gingerly placed the lid back on the tin box. She wanted to run after her dad and tell him how scared she was but she knew it was useless. Then he'd really think she'd lost it. Try to act normal, she told herself. Everything will be all right.

She finally stacked the tin boxes and carried them to the barn. "Dad," she said, "I found some old letters in these boxes. Can I have them?"

"You can have anything you want from the cellar, Cassie. Some of that stuff could go to the historical museum in Alma, if they want it. Your mom might want to save some of it. She's still toying with the idea of selling antiques and there are a few pieces down there that could be refinished. The rest of it will get hauled off to the junkyard, I suppose."

"Do I really get to choose my own room?" Cassie asked.

"Sure, as long as you're fair to Ben. Mom's already staked out the big room with the bay window for us."

Just as she thought. "There are so many rooms up there, can I have the two on the west side and use one for an art studio?"

"I don't see why not, as long as you're willing to clean them. I know how much you love housework." He laughed. "Here, use this rag to clean the dust off those tins and you can take them up there if you like. Take a break. We're heading home in about half an hour anyway."

There was an elegant desk in her room, walnut with carved trim, and a matching chair. She wasn't going to let her mom sell it. It would be a wonderful desk to work at, so much grander than the little crowded one in her room in Topeka.

She looked around. Her room. It didn't feel like hers yet. Maybe it would when they moved out here and she really lived in it, when her art work was on the walls and her bed was over there by the window. That is, if strange things stopped happening.

Cassie dusted off the desk and put the tins on it. Who else had used it? How old was it?

She sat down and opened the first tin, lifted out a bundle of letters and untied the faded red satin ribbon. As she took the top envelope off the stack, she felt something brush past her arm, as though someone were there. The air shimmered slightly as it had earlier. For just an instant, she could see the tall four-poster bed again, and on the desk lay an old nib pen by a letter that began, "Dear Aunt Marie." It was dated April 5, 1897.

"It's my room," said the whispery voice, "My desk. Don't leave me. Read them."

Cassie swung around on the chair, trying to catch a glimpse of whomever was whispering, but could see no one there, just that unsteadiness in the air, almost like the heat waves on the highway that make things in the distance waver. She felt dizzy again as the room returned to the present, empty except for the walnut desk and chair. She tried to get up and run for the door but it was impossible. Icy hands pressed her to the chair, pulled her hand back to the letters.

"Read them," said the voice again.

"Who are you?" Cassie said, her own voice barely croaking out a whisper.

"Just read one letter to me. Please." The cold hands closed around her arm.

With unsteady hands, Cassie took the folded sheet from the envelope. The writing was faded but still readable.

"My Dear Sister," she started. Her voice didn't sound right, as though it were coming from somewhere far away. She cleared her throat. She felt the icy hands release their grip as she nervously began to read. The cold withdrew, almost as though it could gather itself into a ball and move away. Did she dare leave now? She peered around the room. Where was the cold presence?

"Read," the voice whispered, close to her ear. She could feel a cold breath raise the hairs on her neck. Cassie knew she'd never make it to the door. "My Dear Sister Adele," she began again.

Nebraska, February 10, 1887

David and I send you our deepest sympathy for your terrible loss. We pray for the soul of baby John, and for you, that you may find God's peace and the will to go on. How hard it must be to lose your tiny son, barely two years old, to the croup.

Be thankful that Annie is still alive and well. That is a bit of good fortune for which we must thank God. Do not despair. The Lord will watch over you and Johnnie is surely with him in Heaven.

David sends his love. We hope that the next news we hear from you will be happier. The Good Lord willing, perhaps we shall see each other again come summer.

Your loving sister, Marie.

Cassie felt tears pricking at her eyes. She lay the letter slowly on the desk. It was so sad. "Okay, I read the letter," she said. "Who are they?"

There was only silence. The cold presence was gone. Cassie sat slumped in the chair, staring at the letter. A shaft of late afternoon sun shown in on it, lighting up the old writing. 1887. So long ago. But what did it have to do with this house?

She put the letter back in its envelope and closed the tin. She didn't want to read more now. Too many strange things had happened in one afternoon. She bit her lip, feeling uneasy. Would there be more sadness in those letters, so carefully bundled and tied? Would she even want to come back up here to the room that was going to be hers? Would she ever be alone in it?

When she finally got up to leave, her body felt heavy, hard to move. She took the tin that held the letter she had read. Maybe she could read them somewhere else and they'd just be old letters, without any ghost whispering to her. It had to be a ghost. What else could it be?

Jordan's grandmother was right. The house was haunted. But only for me, she thought. Why? she asked, silently, as she tiptoed down the stairs. Why only for me?

"You'll Be Sorry"

I t felt good to be back in her familiar little room in Topeka. Safe. Cassie put the tin of letters on her desk and stared at it. Did she dare open them here? She felt no ghostly presence. She was torn between curiosity and a feeling of dread.

Maybe she'd feel better if she shared them with Jordan. Maybe Jordan would have found out something from her grandmother even though it wasn't Sunday yet. Jordan never was one to be patient. Should she call her or see if she was online? She flipped on her Mac and signed on. Sure enough, there was Jordie in her Buddies List.

"Hey, Jord," she typed, "Didja ask your Granny about my house?"

It always seemed like an interminable wait while Jordan keyed in a reply. Jordie didn't type so great. Cassie eyed the tin of letters and tapped her fingers on the keys impatiently. She could play a whole game of Solitaire waiting for Jordan to answer, and she often did.

"Too much to type. Come over. Hurry!" was the reply that finally appeared on the screen.

Drat. Cassie didn't really feel like going to Jordan's house just now.

"Can't you come over here?"

"Have to stay home til Mom gets back," came the reply.

"OK," Cassie typed. Talking to Jordan anywhere was preferable to being here without her. If there were really much to tell, Jordan would never get it keyed in. Now that she knew there was something to know, Cassie was dying to find out what it was. She didn't bother to turn off the computer. She'd need it later to work on the ghost Indian she was still working on with PhotoShop.

Cassie grabbed the tin of letters and scooted down the stairs and to the kitchen as fast as she could safely go, navigating through Ben's toys and jackets on the hall floor.

"Mom," she called, "I'm going to see Jordan for awhile." When her mom unexpectedly stepped out of her tiny studio, Cassie nearly mowed her down as she rushed past.

"Whoa, wait a minute. What's the rush?" her mother asked. "We just got home a few minutes ago and it isn't long until dinner. Can't you wait until after that? Don't you want to read your mail?"

"Mail? I never get any mail, Mom." Who would write to her when everyone used email, and anyway it wasn't even near her birthday or Christmas. "I'll be back for supper. Just call me when it's ready."

Her mother had a small stack of envelopes in her hand. She held three out to Cassie. "Well, maybe you didn't get mail before, but you certainly do now," she said. "Got a secret admirer?"

Cassie took the envelopes, one pink, one lavender, one white, each carefully addressed in neat printing to Cassie Wade. No return address. Now she was curious -- but still in a hurry to get to Jordan's. "I'll take them with me," she said.

"What, and leave me wondering who they're from?" her mother teased.

"Aw, Mom," Cassie tossed over her shoulder as she headed out the door. "It's probably just a gag from someone at school."

Jordan was waiting for her at the door. "Oh, Cassie," she breathed in a dramatic stage whisper. "It's so cool. An old house with a great big mystery and a ghost and everything!"

Cassie stopped halfway in the door. Okay, so she knew that there was supposed to be a ghost out there. What was this about a mystery? And where did Jordan get off anyway? NOW the house was supposed to be so cool, and before she acted like Cassie's family was crazy to buy it.

Jordan pulled her into the living room. "There might be four ghosts out there, all four of them haunting the place. And there is something hidden, something valuable, but no one's ever found it." She plopped down on the couch. "How come my family never gets involved in anything exciting?"

"Oh, sure, Jordan. When you first heard my parents were buying that place, you didn't think it was so exciting."

"I didn't want you to move away. And I didn't know much about it then. It sounded like an old wreck from what Kevin told us."

Cassie admitted that it had looked like an old wreck, "but not any more. It's a beautiful house. You should see the beveled glass by the front door, and the tower room. I get two rooms all for myself. My own art studio." Why not brag a little?

Jordan was babbling on, excited, "But have you seen a ghost? Do you know who it is?"

Cassie stared at the carpet for a long moment. She put the tin box on the coffee table with the envelopes on top of it.

"It's more like I've felt something. Or hear it," she said in a low voice. "I can't see it, but it wraps itself around me, like something thick. It's so cold! And it whispers.

"Mom told me that they used to call the place Whispering Springs because people heard someone whispering in the wind. No one could tell what the voice said. But I hear it, Jordie. It's scary. The first time I heard it, the whole house changed around me, just for a moment, like I traveled back in time, and it said, 'Can you see it like I saw it?'

"Then when Ben was out at one of the springs I heard it saying, 'Beware, beware.' I heard it again in the cellar when I was helping dad clean it out. The last time was in the room I chose. It made me read an old letter from 1887 I found in the basement. It was a sad letter, about how a baby named John died but at least Annie was well."

Cassie stopped and put her hand to her mouth. Until just that moment, she hadn't made the connection. Annie. The same Annie whose name was on the letter stolen from Miss Mossman? She was sure of it. Who was Annie?

"The ghost TALKS to you?" Jordan shrieked. "JUST to you? Can anyone else hear it? Is it Annie Gwynne?"

"I don't know who it is," Cassie replied. "Who is Annie? I've heard her name in the letter and from Miss Mossman, and now you. No one hears the words but me. Why? That's what I asked the ghost today, 'Why is the house haunted only for me?'"

"We have to find out more about Annie," said Jordan. "Maybe then we'd know."

"I brought the letters with me."

Jordan looked at the old tin with sudden interest. "That's what's in that old box? Cool. Let's read them," she said.

Cassie hesitated. "The ghost wanted me to read them but I hope it won't be upset that I took them home with me. Do you think anything will happen to us if we read them?"

"Good grief, Cassie, they're over a hundred years old! We've never had any ghosts in our house. How will it ever know? Come on, maybe we can find out something. Maybe it IS Annie, or some-one else in her family."

"But who *is* Annie? And you said you had so much to tell me about what your grandmother said. What's this about FOUR ghosts? I want to hear about all that first," Cassie countered.

Jordan leaned forward with excitement. "I went over to see Granny. I couldn't wait till Sunday. She says she used to know the people who lived there, Old Man Cranston and his family. She was even friends with his daughter. He was related to the man that built the house, Joseph Gwynne, but he wasn't his son or anything like that. Granny said Cranston's daughter started seeing and talking to a ghost when she was fourteen. She said it was Annie Gwynne." Jordan stopped and swallowed hard. "We're fourteen, Cassie. Maybe that's why you're the only one who can see and hear her."

"But I'm not even sure it is Annie. Why would she be a ghost?"

"Granny said that the family had a triple tragedy. According to the Cranstons, first Annie's little brother John died. Then his mother died of pneumonia, and finally Annie died, too, all in about twelve years. Joseph Gwynne could not get over their deaths and lived out there like a hermit until he died. He left the place to the Cranstons. I guess they were his closest living relatives.

"There were rumors that Joseph had a secret treasure buried somewhere out there. People tried to find it, but no one ever did. For awhile after Joseph Gwynne died, the Cranstons had a lot of trouble with people sneaking onto the land and digging for it, but after a few years, they gave up.

"After Cranston's daughter grew up and moved away and his wife died, only a few people still told stories about the place being haunted. They said there were four ghosts out there, that all of the Gwynnes were still there protecting his treasure. Adam Cranston hated those stories. He didn't want anyone believing them so he let kids camp out there and welcomed hunters on the land so people wouldn't think anything strange was going on. I guess most people didn't notice anything, but you know what Kevin said about that place the dogs wouldn't go."

"Didn't anyone but Cranston's daughter ever see the ghost?" asked Cassie.

"I don't think so," said Jordan. "Not that my grandmother knew of. And now you. Maybe you have something in common. If you don't find out from the ghost, maybe you could find out from her. The Cranston girl I mean. Well, she's not a girl any more, of course. Granny says she lives in Minnesota. Maybe Granny knows her address."

Cassie swallowed hard. "I don't know whether I WANT to know but I can't stand NOT knowing. It's really creepy hearing voices no one else can hear and feeling that unearthly cold wrap itself around me. If it's Annie, what does she want?"

"Maybe we'll find a clue in the letters," Jordan said. "What are those envelopes on top?"

"I don't know. Mom said they came for me in the mail. I never get mail except for Christmas and my birthday. She teased me about having a secret admirer."

"Well, do you?" Jordan asked.

"If so, it's a big secret to me," Cassie countered. She reached for the three envelopes. "Look, no return address."

She pulled her pocket knife out of her jeans and slit the first one open. It was a card all right, but a very plain one. It looked like someone had made it on a computer. The picture on the front was the outline of a simple white lily with two words in blue,

In Sympathy.

"No way!" Jordan exclaimed. "A SYMPATHY card? Who died?"

Cassie opened the card slowly. Computer printed in a fancy script were two sentences.

Don't move into the old house. You'll be sorry.

That was all.

Cassie let the card fall into her lap. "That is not from a ghost," she whispered.

Jordan grabbed the other two envelopes and took the pocket knife from Cassie. She slit each of them open fast and pulled out the cards. The pink one had a rosy sunrise on the front and the words,

In Time of Sorrow.

Inside, the same graceful writing said,

Sorrow will be all around you in that house.

You have been warned.

Jordan's eyes grew wide. She handed it to Cassie and looked at the third one. This one had a spray of lilacs on it. It said,

In the Loss of Your Loved One

and printed inside,

No one's dead yet. Don't take chances.

Don't leave your brother alone.

You will be contacted. Cooperate.

Cassie and Jordan sat rigid and motionless. The light in the room had grown dim. Jordan reached up and turned on a lamp near the couch.

It was a long time before either of them spoke. Then Cassie turned to her friend. "I bet it's that man who was in the barn, the one I saw looking out the tower window. He wants something and he doesn't want us there. But why? Why does he want to scare me? Why is he threatening Ben? Or is someone else warning me? I have to go home, Jordan. It's getting late and I think I should show these to my mom."

Cassie picked up the cards, the envelopes and the tin of letters and headed out the door. Her feet felt like lead but she had to get home. She had to know Ben was all right.

Treasure the Irises

en was playing video games in the family room. Dinner smelled great. Everything seemed fine at home. How could things be so normal and so frightening at the same time? She rushed over to her mom, who was sketching while her dad was finishing dinner. She dropped the cards right onto the sketch pad, not even thinking or caring whether it would annoy her mother. "It's not my imagination," she said. "See?"

"What's not your imagination, Cassie?" her mother asked. She looked down at the cards and frowned. "Are these the cards you got in the mail today?" She opened the first one. Cassie had dropped them in the same order she and Jordan had opened them.

Her mother smiled as though she were looking at a bad joke. "I guess someone wants to revive the old rumors about the place," she said. The second one brought a frown. The third one brought her to her feet and to the kitchen doorway.

"This is not funny!" she exclaimed. "This is no way to joke. Daniel, look at this." She shoved the cards into his hands. He read them and shrugged.

"No, it's not funny, but it's nothing to worry about. It's probably just some kids playing pranks because of the old stories about the house."

"But these are threatening notes, Daniel, especially about Ben."

"If someone were really trying to threaten us, don't you think they would have sent something to US and not to Cassie?" he answered. "What would anyone who was really trying to scare us off hope to accomplish by sending notes to her?"

It sounded logical but Cassie wasn't reassured. Until she read the cards, she had been so focused on the ghost that she had nearly forgotten that there was someone real and alive watching them, someone she thought was dangerous. Now she had two frightening entities to deal with and no one believed her except Jordan. For all she knew, they were working together, the man and the ghost. She resolved not to let Ben out of her sight when they were at Whispering Springs, even if she knew that was an impossible task.

After dinner, Cassie put the dishes in the dishwasher and started it. She hadn't said a word during dinner and she didn't feel like talking now. Sure, Ben was trouble sometimes, but he was an okay little brother. If no one else was going to protect him, she'd have to try.

The first thing she needed was information. There was nowhere to turn tonight but the letters in the tin, and they were so old, how could they lead her to anything helpful? She had to start somewhere, do something, so as soon as she was done in the kitchen, she tiptoed up the stairs to her room with the letters and quietly shut her door.

She had forgotten that she left her computer on. She ought to check her email, she thought, without much enthusiasm. Usually she had a bunch of messages. Tonight there was just one. She didn't recognize the email address and there was no name with it and no subject. When she clicked on it, a photo of the house at Whispering Springs appeared. To her horror, there she was sitting on the front porch and Ben was digging in the dirt with a stick. She knew her parents had not taken that photo. It was when Ben found the iris brooch and gave it to her. Who took that picture? Under it was this message:

"Do not cross me. Do not get in my way. Do not talk to anyone about this. My warnings are real. I will stop at nothing. There is something I want at the ranch. You will help me find it. Cooperate or the warnings on the cards will come true. You will be watched. Your instructions will come from me by email. Do not fail to read and follow them."

Cassie stared at the screen for a long time, unable to move. She was right. He did want something and now he wanted her to help him. Someone on the inside. He probably didn't dare to go into the house as much now that her parents were there often and had reported him to the sheriff.

He knew where she lived. He knew her email address. He was watching her. Her and Ben. Her mind went over and over it. It was hard to think. How did he know those things?

Dimly, she remembered Kevin saying you could find out all sorts of things on the internet, or by asking a few people simple questions and building on the answers. The man had her family's name and her mom's cell phone number. Maybe that was all it took. Maybe he found out more by watching them.

The hair on the back of her neck prickled. She couldn't stand the thought of someone watching her. And now he expected her to help him find something at Whispering Springs. What could he possibly want out there? That hidden treasure no one ever found? Was it real? She thought a long time. Then she clicked "Reply," and typed,

"I can't help you find something if I don't know what it is. What do you want? Leave Ben alone."

Then, although she was sure it wouldn't do any good, and though for all she knew the ghost and the Spy were on the same side, she added,

"If you think you can get away with anything at Whispering Springs, you can't. The ghosts will stop you."

She hoped Jordan's idea that they were protecting

Gwynne's treasure was right.

She was so scared after she sent the email that she didn't go back downstairs. She might not be able to resist telling her parents what had happened, and she had been warned not to do that. Besides, she didn't want to frighten Ben. Part of her thought she should tell her parents anyway, but the other part believed the threats and she didn't dare.

She was much too nervous to draw or paint. Her hands wouldn't stop shaking. After staring at the screen far too long, she finally decided to read the letters. At least she might learn something more about Whispering Springs.

The letters were interesting but none of them told her anything about secrets, buried treasure, or ghosts. All of them were from someone named Marie to someone named Adele, just like the first one she read, and they were all written in the years 1887-1893. They were carefully bundled in neat little packets by year and date.

Marie and Adele were sisters and Adele was Annie Gwynne's mother. Marie lived in Nebraska and they hardly ever got to see each other. The trip was too difficult over bad roads in those days and it was a long trip by train. Marie was busy on the farm and raising her daughters. Her oldest daughter, Dora, was about three years younger than Annie.

The letters made it clear that Adele's life had been sad after baby John died. Even though she still had Annie and loved her dearly, her husband Joseph could not get over the boy's death. In the last letter, when Annie would have been ten years old, Marie suggested that Adele bring her to Nebraska for the summer. Surely Joseph could manage without them for two months, and money was not a problem, was it? Maybe they'd be happier there for awhile. Cassie wondered whether that was why the letters stopped. Had they gone to Nebraska? She wished she had the other boxes of letters here, too.

When she finished reading, Cassie noticed how quiet the house was. It was after midnight. Everyone had gone to bed long ago. No one had even knocked on her door to say goodnight. They must have thought she had fallen asleep hours before and didn't want to wake her. Not likely I'd be asleep, she said to herself. Not tonight.

She stuck her hand in her jeans pocket to touch her lucky stone. She always carried it, a smooth lump of malachite. Would it really bring her any luck now? Kind of a childish idea, really. Instead of the stone, her fingers found the iris brooch. She remembered the fancy lettering on the back. She hadn't been able to read it before, but maybe with some silver polish it would be readable.

She sneaked quietly down the stairs, turned on the light over the kitchen sink and found the silver polish and a soft rag. It took a lot of rubbing to get the years of tarnish off the pin. It was more beautiful and ornate than she thought. The letters began to show up and she rubbed harder. She didn't know why it felt so important to her. It certainly wasn't going to save her from the Spy. He was spying on them, and that's what she was going to call him, at least until she knew his name.

When she had polished the piece as much as she could, she looked at it under a bright light. She was so surprised she almost cried out. On the brooch in very tiny and graceful script was engraved,

For Annie, May 24, 1893
Tenth Birthday
Treasure the Irises.
Your Loving Mother

Cassie was holding Annie's birthday gift, and her birthday was the same date as Cassie's. She felt goose bumps crawling up her arms again. Why did Annie haunt her? How could she live at Whispering Springs with a Spy and a ghost? Which one was more dangerous?

Cassie wished it weren't one o'clock in the morning. She wanted to call Jordan. She wanted it to be morning. She wished it were all just a bad dream, but there she was, holding Annie's birthday gift and scared to even check her own email.

Meet Me in the Graveyard

She must have gone to bed and fallen asleep somehow because that's where she woke up when her mother called her.

"Cassie, come down to breakfast, Honey. It's late, but we all slept in this morning. I made some blueberry muffins and cheesy eggs, just like you like them."

She sounded so cheery. Nothing to be afraid of at all. Just some prankster sending cards. That's what THEY thought.

Cassie dragged herself out of bed and pulled on a robe. She'd eat before she lost her appetite and shower and dress later. She was amazed that she even felt like eating, but those muffins smelled wonderful. Again she marveled that when some things were so out of whack, other things were perfectly ordinary. Her grandmother always said that things look better after you sleep on them. It seemed she was right.

Nothing looked all that menacing with the sun streaming in the windows and everyone gathered around the table for breakfast. Ben was wearing his cowboy hat and sheriff's star. He jabbered on and on about wanting a horse and how much space there was in the barn. For once he didn't even mention ghosts or werewolves.

Cassie could see her mom and dad sneaking glances at her, wondering whether she was all right after the threatening "sympathy" cards last night. They don't have a clue, she thought.

It wasn't as hard to act normal as she thought it would be because everything SEEMED normal. If she thought about last night she got butterflies in her stomach, but she did her best to think of other things. Like the mosaic she was working on at school, or her ghost Indian, or the cathedral model she was building for her history project. Or that cute new guy in her Spanish class, Jeff. She couldn't entirely keep her mind off the Spy, but she told herself that the way to stay safe was to be sure that she and Ben were not far from their parents and that Ben was never alone. What did the Spy think he was going to do to Ben anyway?

"Penny for your thoughts?" her mother asked.

Cassie could tell her mother hoped to hear something safe and familiar, so she obliged. "I was thinking about my cathedral project," she answered. "I have to spend some time on it this weekend."

"That's fine. You and Ben can stay here today. Our electrical contractor surprised us by saying he could finish the rewiring out at the house today. It was either do it today or wait another three weeks, so Dad and I grabbed the chance. We need to be out there, but you and Ben can stay here. We'll be back by supper time."

Was it safe for her parents to be there? It always was before. Was it safe for her and Ben to be home alone, even in the city? Where would the Spy be watching? At Whispering Springs or here in town? Cassie didn't know which place would be safer.

She tried to analyze it. Her mind didn't want to deal with thoughts of danger but she forced herself to try to think like she thought the Spy might. Of course he didn't want her parents suspecting anything. He would probably make sure they never saw him. He had to have known that they'd see the sympathy cards but he must have counted on them thinking they were a prank. That would make it easier for them to discount her being scared of other stuff. Oh, yeah, Cassie's just spooked by those silly cards and a dusty old house. Crazy kid.

And he was counting on her help. He couldn't very well expect her parents to help him find what-ever he wanted out at Whispering Springs. So, if she was figuring right, her parents were safe enough. Probably she and Ben were, too, as long as she didn't "cross him," as he so nastily put it. Since he was most interested in what went on out there, he probably would be watching at Whispering Springs, not here. She let out a long sigh. She hadn't realized how tense she was, that she had been holding her breath. She felt a little safer now, for the time being.

Later that morning after her parents left, Cassie

started thinking about characters in books and movies, how they always did just exactly the wrong thing in a dangerous situation, like not turning on the light in a dark house, or going back to look at something instead of just leaving. How could she be smarter?

Should she check her email or not? It was like some awful fascination in a horror movie. She was scared what she might find, but she could hardly stand not knowing if the Spy had answered her. And she would *have* to check it if she was going to "cooperate" and protect Ben.

For awhile, Cassie pretended she wasn't even going to look. She baked a batch of brownies, played checkers with Ben, and worked on her cathedral. Finally she got her sketch pad, intending to draw Ben in his cowboy outfit, but when she looked down she saw that she had started sketching outlines of the house at Whispering Springs. She dropped the sketch pad to the floor.

"Hey, Cassie, what's the matter?" asked Ben, looking up from the Lego castle he was building.

"Nothing, Ben," she choked out. "I just didn't like my drawing. I'm going to get online. Want to come upstairs and look at my rock collection?" Ordinarily, Ben begged to look at it and she wouldn't let him. Now she had to figure out how to keep him in sight.

"Okay," he said, "but can I go over to Matt's house later?"

"Maybe," she said, trying to figure out how to keep him with her.

Upstairs in her room, she handed Ben the treasure box of her favorite rocks without even admonishing him to be careful with it and keep things in order. She was just glad he was with her. For once she was happy to share it.

Online. She'd never been afraid to connect before. While she waited for her password to be verified, she fingered the iris brooch. It was so beautiful. Over a hundred years old and it belonged to a dead girl who had the same birthday she did. And now, she might be a ghost.

The screen changed and her email Inbox appeared. There were a bunch of messages, some from kids at school and one from the strange address of the Spy. Cassie took a deep breath. She might as well go right to that one. She wouldn't be able to think about the others anyway. As she clicked on it, she closed her eyes tight and said a silent prayer. Please, God, don't let him hurt my family. Don't let him hurt Ben.

The words leapt out at her from the screen.

Don't play games with me, kid. You don't ask the questions. Do as you are told and keep your mouth shut if you care about your brother. You can't do anything for me in town. Make sure you are out at the house tomorrow, with or without your parents. Meet me in the graveyard. Alone.

Cassie hunched down on her chair, hands gripping

her crossed arms, as she read the words over and over. She could hardly breathe. What had she expected? That the Spy would be scared by the ghost? That he'd leave her alone? One thing was for sure, she wasn't going to answer this message!

"Cassie, what's this green one?"

She jumped at the sound of Ben's voice and let out a strangled sound. Her concentration on the message was so complete she had forgotten he was there. She quickly clicked on the next message, hoping Ben hadn't read anything on screen.

"Cassie, what's the matter?" Ben hopped off the bed and stood solemnly by her chair.

She couldn't very well tell him "nothing," not after acting like she'd just seen a snake under her desk. She let out a long breath, trying to make it slow and steady.

"It's okay, Ben," she said softly, trying to sound as though it were. "I just read a message that wasn't very nice. I was thinking about it and you startled me. That's all."

"What did it say?" he asked, his eyes big and concerned.

She didn't answer at first. What could she say? Cassie didn't like lying and she hated it when someone lied to her. The best she could do was to be evasive and hope Ben would accept it. She didn't want to scare him, too.

"Someone wants me to do something I don't want to do and says bad things will happen if I don't," she finally said. "But don't worry, Ben. I won't do anything bad and everything will be all right." Thank goodness he was eight years old. If she'd said that to Jordan, she never would have gotten away with it. Jordie would have pestered her forever until she told everything.

Maybe Ben could accept that and go back to looking at the rocks, but Cassie went over and over the words in her mind,

Keep your mouth shut if you care about your brother. . . . . Meet me in the graveyard. Alone.

Be at the Truck

Cassie didn't know how she got through the rest of the afternoon. She was never so relieved to see her parents pull into the driveway in her life. She only half listened when they told her that the house now had wonderful lighting, including the track lighting she wanted in her studio room, how great it looked, how there were plenty of outlets for computers and all their other electronic stuff.

They were beaming about the house, how fast it was shaping up, how beautiful it was. Her mother loved the chandeliers in the living room and dining room. There were even telephones there now. They thought they could take the family out there over the weekend in just a week. Already. Cassie couldn't remember when she'd seen them so enthusiastic.

Dad was all ecstatic over the carved oak woodwork. "The workmanship on the interior panels around the front door is superb."

Obviously, they hadn't seen anything frightening out there. No ghost. No Spy. She wished there were some way to tell them what was happening -- and that they'd believe it -- but she didn't dare.

It wasn't until she dimly heard them say they weren't going out to Whispering Springs the next day that she sat up straight, eyes wide, and paid attention for real. They were taking a day off. After church, Mom was going to paint. Not house painting, she said with a laugh, but something creative, maybe something she'd be proud to put over that beautiful mantle. And she'd make something special for dinner since it was her turn to cook. Dad was going fishing with a friend.

Cassie swallowed hard, remembering the words,

Make sure you are out at the house tomorrow, with or without your parents.

How was she supposed to get there? What would happen if she didn't? Could she just answer the Spy's email after all, and tell him she couldn't come? Not likely he'd accept that. Maybe he KNEW her parents weren't going out there on Sunday. Maybe he'd been spying on them the whole time today, listening in on their conversations. She bit her thumbnail, something she hadn't done in over a year, chewed it down to the quick. Even if she could get out there, how could she face the Spy in the graveyard with her parents way back in Topeka?

Cassie swallowed hard. Her arms and legs felt weak, as though no amount of effort on her part could move them. She looked at her right hand and willed it to move, watched as it slowly turned over, palm up. Okay, she could move if she really tried.

But would she make it to her room?

She barely heard her parents talk about ordering a pizza and Ben whooping his approval. A voice she recognized as hers, though it sounded tiny and breathless, was asking, "Mom, can I go over to Jordan's for a little while?"

"No fair," shouted Ben. "We had to stay home all day and I wanted to go to Matt's house."

"All right, Cassie, but come home in half an hour," her mom said. "Ben, I'm sorry you didn't get to go to Matt's. You two can get together tomorrow."

Cassie stopped in her tracks, which wasn't hard at the slow speed she was moving. Would Ben be okay tomorrow? She assured herself he'd be fine, because if she found a way to get to Whispering Springs, the Spy would be waiting for her, and Ben would be safe in Topeka. Besides, that awful man wouldn't do anything bad to her as long as he needed her to "cooperate." She dragged her feet toward the back door. Pizza. How could they think of eating?

At Jordan's, she mustered up the strength to lift the door knocker. Why couldn't they get the doorbell fixed anyway? No one came. She banged again. She HAD to talk to Jordan.

Kevin finally answered the door. "Hey, Cassie," he said, "Come on in. Jordie's playing video games with Lisa. Have to keep her occupied 'til Mom gets back from the store."

"Please, Kevin, can you play with Lisa for a few

minutes? I only have a little time and I HAVE to talk to Jordan right now."

"Whoa, what's the big deal?" he asked. "Don't pass out on me. Take a deep breath. You don't look so good. Is everything all right?"

"Just PLEASE let me talk to Jordan," she begged.

"No problem," he said, heading for the family room.

A minute later Jordan appeared. "Cassie, you look terrible. What's wrong?"

"I have to get to Whispering Springs tomorrow and Mom and Dad aren't going. I got email from that man who sent the cards. He's making more threats, says I can't tell anyone, but I had to tell SOMEONE who would believe me. I have to meet him in the graveyard out there tomorrow. Alone. What am I going to do?"

Jordan stared, not moving.

Didn't her best friend believe her? Just when her knees were about to crumple under her, Jordan put both hands on her shoulders, turned her around, and pushed her to the kitchen and onto a chair. Then she handed Cassie a glass of water.

"Drink," she ordered. "Then take ten deep breaths before you say another thing." She pulled a chair out and sat facing Cassie.

Cassie did as she was told, relieved that someone was taking charge.

"What did the email say?" Jordan asked.

Cassie started to talk and only a squeak of fear

came out. Jordan reached out and took her hands and held on. How did Jordan always know just what to do to calm people down? After a few more sips of water and slow breaths, Cassie was finally able to talk almost normally.

"He sent two emails. I read them so many times I could never forget them. He said, 'do as you are told and keep your mouth shut if you care about your brother. Make sure you are out at the house tomorrow, with or without your parents. Meet me in the graveyard. Alone.' What am I going to do, Jordan?" she asked.

"Kevin will take you. That is, he'll take US," she said. "But we'll have to tell him why."

"But that Spy said not to tell anyone," Cassie objected.

"You already told me," Jordan pointed out, "and you have to get to Whispering Springs. I don't see what choice you have. You got any other way to get out there?"

Cassie admitted she didn't. "But I'm scared. What if he finds out I told? What might happen to me? Or you and Kevin? Or Ben?"

"If you don't go out there and meet him, what do you think will happen then?" countered Jordan. "You'd better go see what he wants."

"But he said I had to come alone," said Cassie.

"He said you had to come to the graveyard alone," Jordan said. "He knows you'd have to come out there with someone or you'd never get there.

But we have to go right after lunch because I have to go to my grandmother's house for dinner at 6:30. I'm going to get Kevin. We have to plan everything carefully."

Cassie said a silent thank you for having a friend like Jordan. That would be the worst part of moving, being so many miles away from her. Beyond that, her mind nearly shut down from panic.

When Jordan came back with Kevin, she pointed to a chair and said, "Sit."

Kevin looked amused at Jordan's peremptory tone. "Okay, okay, so I'm sitting. What's the big emergency?"

Jordan rattled off the details as fast as she could talk. Kevin's eyebrows raised. You couldn't blame him for being skeptical.

"Tell him, Cassie," Jordan ordered. "Make him believe us."

Cassie just burst into tears.

"Hey, Cassie, don't take it so hard," Kevin said. "Is what Jordan is saying true?"

She nodded. "I have to get to Whispering Springs tomorrow." It was all she could get out.

Kevin looked at Jordan and raised his eyebrows. "You up for this?" he asked.

"Yes," she said.

"Okay, Cassie. Be at my truck at 2:00," he said. "Wear shoes you can run in, just in case."

The Graveyard

ow had she made it through dinner? How could pizza be tasteless? What even happened at church or lunch? How had she gotten through twenty hours of waiting? Obsession. Now she knew what it meant. She couldn't think of anything else but meeting the Spy. Even Annie and the ghost were far from her mind.

She found herself standing by Kevin's beat up old truck at 1:55 p.m., grateful that Mom hadn't objected when she said she and Jordan were going rock hounding with Kevin. She wished that was what they were really doing.

Kevin and Jordan were there right on time. Jordan on time. That had to be a first.

"Ready to go rock hounding?" Kevin asked. He gave Cassie a half smile.

They hardly said a word the whole way out to the ranch except when Cassie asked Kevin if there really was a place the hunting dogs wouldn't go.

Kevin pursed his lips. "Yeah. It was real strange. We were walking along the creek by this giant dead tree that looked like it had been hit by lightning a

long time ago and the dogs just whimpered and
stopped. We tried to get them to walk past it and
they wouldn't. We finally had to take them back the
way we came. Some of the guys got kind of
spooked. I mean, the dogs were acting so weird, and
then there was that whispering sound, like someone
was trying to talk to us. We couldn't see anyone or
make out the words. I'll show you the place some-
time if you really want to see it, but I'd stay away
from there if I were you."

Cassie didn't reply. Her heart was pounding.
Maybe the dogs sensed the Spy was lurking somewhere near the tree. Or something else. Kevin and
his friends heard the voice! Whispering Springs. It
didn't sound like a pleasant place any more. It
sounded dangerous.

She wondered whether she would make it out of
the truck and up the trail to the graveyard. Alone.
Jordan and Kevin were great, but they couldn't do
that with her. To make sure their story held up, they
were going to actually go rock hounding. Kevin
said there was a good place not far from the house.
They'd all meet there when Cassie could get away.
If she got away, she thought.

Kevin stopped the truck just inside the turn-in to
Whispering Springs. He dug something out of his
pocket and handed her a whistle. "Take this," he
said. "Blow it if you're in danger. I can hear it where
we'll be checking out the rocks." When she looked
quizzical, he said, "I take it hunting. Just keep it

with you. My deer rifle is in the truck. We'll be right here, Cassie."

She forced herself to walk up the gravel drive, wondering where the man was, whether he was watching her now. Even if Kevin and Jordan were close enough to come if she needed them, she had to face the Spy alone. Cassie straightened her shoulders and thought of Ben. She had to do it for Ben. She was trembling all over but she made straight for the graveyard.

When she got as far as the spring she felt in her pocket for the whistle and looked toward the cemetery. She didn't see anyone waiting there. Was he hiding? Would she have to wait for him to come? Whispering Springs. Here she was. Would she hear anything this time?

As Cassie headed toward the low stone wall that surrounded the graveyard, a sudden cold wind swirled around her as though she was caught in some invisible whirlpool. Freezing fingers gripped her wrists and pulled her toward the tombstones. She tried to wrench her hands away and couldn't. Cassie panicked. She tried to run. It was useless.

Surely she was imagining the whispered words in her ears. She tried to block out everything but the feel of her feet dragging toward the tombstones but the whispering became more insistent, louder and more distinct. Her wrists hurt.

What if there were no "Spy"? What if the man in the barn really was just a tramp and was gone?

Maybe this strange entity that whispered had somehow lured her out here. How? For what?

The chill wrapped itself around her and propelled her toward the graves. She fought it, staggering on the weed-choked, rocky path, shivering from both the cold that enveloped her and her fear. She remembered the whistle in her pocket and wondered whether blowing it would help, whether she could even get it out.

Cassie stumbled through an opening in the low stone wall and into the small overgrown graveyard. Near a tombstone, the force calmed and released her wrists. Cassie caught her breath. She thought she saw a slight shimmer in the air, and within it, a hazy figure.

The whispering grew to a hiss in her ears. Don't listen, she told herself, but there was no way to block it out. At first she only heard, "Beware, beware." It startled her when the words changed. "Don't move," it said. "Stay there if you want to be safe."

Cassie had spent two days in terror over meeting the Spy here but she had never expected to be threatened by this invisible force, by the voice of Whispering Springs. She struggled to comprehend. Where was the Spy? Was he coming? Was this what she really should be afraid of?

Then Cassie looked at the grave stone. She gasped. It was worn and hard to read, but Cassie could still make out the words. She read, in a hoarse whisper,

Annie Katherine Gwynne
Born May 24, 1883
Died June 16, 1897
Beloved daughter of Joseph and Adele,
Struck down and taken from me.
Now is the end of all my joy.
May the angels protect her forevermore.

Annie's grave. She was standing on Annie's grave, and something had forced her there, whispering warnings -- or were they threats? The stone was topped by a white marble angel, wings spread, hair flowing, a wreath of carved flowers in her hair. She was beautiful even with the years of discoloration and lichen growing on her. Did the angels protect Annie? What was going to protect her, Cassie?

She turned her back to the angel, knees weak, and slumped to the ground. Her throat was dry. She rubbed her aching wrists. She had used up all the energy she had coming this far.

The whispered words were softer now, harder to make out. She caught a word here and there, "Stay there . . . Don't move . . . Beware."

Time seemed to stop. It felt as though she had been there, sitting on Annie's grave, for hours but it couldn't have been more than ten minutes.

She heard a rustling in the grass behind her. She stood up, wobbly, and tried to turn around, but not fast enough. Powerful arms grabbed her from behind and held her.

"At least you know how to follow instructions," the man's voice said. "That's good. Do as I say and you and your brother will be safe."

Cassie was surprised. She thought the Spy would have a rough voice, but he sounded calm. In control. "Don't ask any questions. Just listen. There is a treasure hidden on this property. I want it, and you're going to see to it that I get it."

"But how?" Cassie blurted out. "I don't know where it is. How can I get it?"

He shook her. "Shut up. Your parents must know about it. Why else would they buy the old place? But they haven't found it yet, have they?"

"Let me go," Cassie said. "I'll listen." Maybe she could at least see what he looked like. She was surprised her voice worked and that she actually used it.

"Fat chance," he said, tightening his grip on her shoulders. "Now here's what you do. I know you already found some old letters. There is a clue in a letter somewhere. You find that letter and give it to me. Tell no one. Send me email. I'll be in touch. Work fast."

Defiantly, Cassie answered, "And what if I don't? What if I can't?"

The man moved his hands to her neck and began to squeeze. Cassie coughed and choked.

"Don't mess with me, kid. I could wring your neck like a chicken."

Just then a terrifying shriek pierced the air and a

fierce gust of wind shot across the graveyard, blasting the Spy from behind. Startled, he let Cassie go and whirled around.

Cassie ran, the sound of the earsplitting scream following her down the path.

Winona

Cassie didn't remember pulling the whistle out of her pocket and blowing it as she ran. She didn't remember looking back to see whether someone or something was following her. Terror gave her speed. She passed the house and ran down the long drive toward the road.

Jordan and Kevin were running toward her, summoned by the whistle.

"Cassie," Jordan yelled, "Are you all right?"

Cassie nearly ran on past them. She was scared to stop, scared at what might be coming behind her. Kevin grabbed her and held her.

"Calm down, Cassie," he said. "We're here. There's no one behind you."

Jordan hugged her. "It's okay, Cassie. You're safe. It's really okay. Isn't it?" she asked, concern in her voice. "What was that horrible scream?"

Cassie looked at them, wild-eyed. She hung onto them. Safe. She was safe. From what? She couldn't speak.

Kevin and Jordan helped Cassie into the truck and Jordan handed her a can of juice. Cassie knew

Jordan was about to do her "take ten deep breaths and take a drink" routine, so she waved her hand in front of her face to show she knew and started working to slow her breathing. It helped.

"What happened, Cassie?" Jordan asked. "Did that guy harm you?"

"No, not really. He sneaked up and grabbed me from behind so I couldn't see him. He told me what he wanted, and when I asked what would happen if I couldn't or didn't do it, he started to choke me. To show me what he would do to Ben or to me if I don't cooperate, I guess. He said he could wring my neck like a chicken!" She took another deep breath to steady herself.

"Just then a freezing gust of wind came out of nowhere. It was like it was aimed at him and not me. At the same time, there was a deafening scream, like something that was trying to terrify the world, and he let go of me. I ran. Oh, Jordan, what am I going to do?" Cassie huddled close to her friend.

"The first thing we're going to do is head for home," Kevin said. "No sense hanging around here to see if that guy does decide to come after you. I don't think he will, but I'm not waiting to find out." He started the truck and turned it around.

They rode in silence for a few moments.

Memories started coming back to Cassie. "That wasn't all that happened," she said. "When I was walking to the cemetery, almost there, I felt that cold wrap itself around me again, but this time there was something more. There were freezing hands clenching my wrists. They pulled me to Annie Gwynne's grave. The whispering voice said to stay there if I wanted to be safe."

"Was it threatening you?"

"I don't know. That's what I thought, that maybe this force was working with that awful man, especially when it made me go to the graveyard and told me to stay there. But now I'm not sure. If it was on his side, why did it make him let me go? How can that even happen, a wind that can point itself at someone like a weapon?"

"Maybe it was protecting you," Jordan offered.

"I wonder," said Cassie. "There was one other time I heard that scream; that first day when Ben and I wanted to go into the house. Something slammed the door shut and shrieked. It scared us out of going in, and just after that I saw the man in the tower window."

"Then why didn't it scare you AWAY from the cemetery this time?" Jordan asked.

"I don't know," Cassie replied. "Maybe it knew I had to go there to keep Ben safe."

"It must be Annie's ghost, like I told you before," Jordan insisted.

"But if it's Annie, why would she act like this? Jordan, she has the same birthday as me," Cassie said. "She was only fourteen years old when she died, just our age. Her tombstone said something about being struck down and taking all the joy from life. There is a beautiful marble angel on her grave stone, and the words said the angels should protect her forever. Why didn't they protect her when she was fourteen? What happened to her?"

They were driving down I-70 now. Cassie envied all the people in the cars and trucks on the highway. People leading normal lives. People not haunted by ghosts or threatened by dangerous strangers.

"And who ever heard of a ghost blowing around like a whirlwind in broad daylight? So far, I haven't even been out at Whispering Springs at night. Maybe it's even worse."

"But you're the only one who feels the presence, or force, or whatever you want to call it, right?" Kevin asked.

"Yes, and I'm the only one who has seen the Spy or heard from him, too," Cassie said.

"There must be a connection," Jordan said, "But what?"

"Did the man tell you what he wanted?" Kevin asked.

"He said there is a treasure, just like the old rumors said. He must have been looking for it the day I saw him in the tower room. Maybe that's why he was camping in the barn. He thinks my parents know about it and that's why they bought the place. They don't, or at least they never told me and Ben about it. He says there is a clue in a letter and I have to find it and get it to him."

"A letter, like those old letters you brought over

to my house?" Jordan asked.

"I guess so, but I read all the letters in that box and there was nothing about any treasure in them. There are some more boxes of letters in the house, though. The ghost told me to read the letters. If it is Annie, maybe she knows about a letter with a clue in it. Maybe that's why she told me to read them. But what if it isn't there? And what if it is? What kind of treasure could it be?"

Jordan turned to Kevin. "We're going straight to Grandma's house," she ordered. "She's the only one who can tell us anything about it. We're supposed to be there in an hour anyway. Let's just call Mom from there and let her know we decided to visit Granny early."

"I can't invite myself for dinner," Cassie protested weakly. Dinner or no dinner, she badly wanted to talk with Jordan's grandmother.

"Granny won't mind a bit," said Jordan, "but if your parents don't want you to stay, Kevin can run you home after we talk." She pulled a canvas bag from beneath her feet. "Look, we even got some rocks. Real rock hounds. No one needs to know what happened unless you want to tell them."

Jordan's grandmother was in the middle of cooking dinner, but when Jordie did a fast explanation of why they were there early, carefully leaving out any mention of the Spy or the meeting in the graveyard, she looked Cassie straight in the eye.

"Come here, honey," she said. She wrapped her

arms around Cassie and lead her to the couch. "You sit right here while I get that pan of lasagna in the oven. Seems to me Jordan is leaving out a lot, but I think I can help you."

When she returned a few minutes later, she was carrying an old composition notebook. Stuffed into it were a few letters. She sat down next to Cassie.

"When your parents bought the old Cranston place, I wondered whether all would go well. You see, I grew up on a ranch near there. Winona Cranston and I were best friends. She was just about my age and her father was the one you call 'Old Man Cranston.'

"The year she turned fourteen, she started to feel and see strange things in and around the old house. For years, everyone had heard whispering sounds that no one could understand, but Winona suddenly could. It gave her the creeps. She said sometimes she would catch sight of a faint image of someone, a girl about her age. She seemed to be searching for something. When she told her parents about it, they didn't believe her."

"Just like me!" Cassie broke in.

"So it seems," Granny continued. "Her father, Adam Cranston, inherited the place in 1940 when Joseph Gwynne died. There were family stories passed down about ghosts and a treasure, but since no one had seen a ghost and a treasure never was found, nobody, including Winona's father believed any of it. He was annoyed every time someone brought it up. He had a lot of trouble keeping treasure hunters off the place after he first got it. People would show up with shovels. Can you imagine? They'd sneak in at night and even dig in the graveyard. You'd have thought they didn't know or care that it was private property, like they could just dig up something and make off with it.

"When Winona started understanding the voice, her parents still refused to believe the old stories might be true. They thought she was losing her mind and threatened to send her away to a boarding school. I guess they thought that if she was far away from Whispering Springs, she wouldn't be influenced by the stories.

"Winona didn't want to go so she stopped talking about her experiences, except with me. I wrote some of them down in this notebook. The letters are some she sent to me after we grew up and she moved away. We spent many hours trying to figure out the truth about Whispering Springs, even after we were grown and married, but we never did.

"What we did learn was this. Joseph Gwynne somehow got his hands on a lot of money. He didn't come from a rich family, but when he came back to this area in about 1878, he had enough money to buy the ranch and build that big house. He married a beautiful young schoolteacher named Adele who came from Nebraska. They had two children named Annie and John. Both of them died. Johnnie died first, of some disease like whooping cough, I think."

"It was the croup," said Cassie. "I read about it in a letter from Adele's sister Marie. But what happened to Annie?"

"She was struck by lightning, on the hill above the creek. One of the old women in church told Winona that Annie was killed when she ran away from her father in a terrible thunderstorm. He never forgave himself. Her mother died of pneumonia four years before that, so Annie was all he had left."

"Why did she run away from him?" Cassie asked.

"No one knows. Annie couldn't tell anyone, and Joe Gwynne never did. He lived like a hermit after her funeral, hardly ever leaving home. He lost contact with Adele's family, wouldn't answer their letters. He refused to get a telephone. No one knew whether he still had a lot of money or had spent it all.

"Winona always wondered whether anyone would hear from Annie again. As far as we know, no one has until now. But then, there haven't been any girls your age out on the old place in all these years.

"Winona married and moved to Minnesota. After her parents died, she didn't want the house. Too many bad memories. She discovered that the county was taking it for back taxes. You'd think she would have paid the taxes and tried to sell it for more, but her husband convinced her that they couldn't get much for it in that run-down condition. It's lucky for the old house that your parents want to fix it up."

"But it's so frightening now," said Cassie. "How can I ever live there?"

"I'm sure it's disturbing, Cassie, but I don't think Annie will harm you. She wants something from you, wants to be with you. She wouldn't risk that by hurting you, but perhaps you need to find out more from Winona. Is there something else going on out there that might really be dangerous?"

Cassie closed her eyes. She couldn't tell another person. She couldn't take the risk. She wasn't going to lie, either. "I can't tell you," she said.

"Honey, if you're in some kind of danger, you come to me. I'll do what I can." She looked at Cassie. "There is something else going on. I just know it. You be careful."

"I will," Cassie said. She had never meant anything more in her life.

"If you think it would help, you can take this notebook home and read it. You'll find Winona's street and email addresses, if you'd like to ask her any questions. I'd love to have you stay for dinner, but I have a feeling it would be very awkward for you with so many people here. It's up to you, dear."

Cassie took the notebook gratefully. "Thanks, Mrs. Dexter. I don't think I'm ready for a dinner with a lot of people. And thank you for all the information."

"You're welcome, Cassie. You'll call me if I can do anything, won't you?" She peered intently into Cassie's eyes.

Cassie knew she was looking for a clue about what was really going on. It wasn't long ago she was hoping for someone to believe her. She knew Granny Dexter would, and it was all she could do to keep from telling her. I have to think of Ben, she kept telling herself. And me. It was my neck the Spy had his hands on, she thought, shuddering. She never wanted to feel his hands again.

The Notebook

hen Kevin dropped her off at home with a bag of rocks and the notebook tucked inside, Cassie trudged up to the door, trying hard to look nonchalant.

"Hi, Mom," she called.

Ben came running. "Hey, Cas," he hollered. "Got any rocks for me?"

"Sure, Ben," she said, relieved that the ruse was working. She dug a piece of quartzite out of the bag, a nice one. "Here, this one is for you. Isn't it nice and sparkly?"

Ben held it up to the light. "It might be a magic rock." He rubbed it experimentally. Nothing happened. "You probably need the right spell," he said.

"Probably," agreed Cassie. Thank goodness he was safe and the same as ever.

Her mother appeared in the kitchen doorway, wooden spoon in one hand, licking the fingers of the other one. "Mmmm, nothing beats home made lemon meringue pie filling. Want some before it all goes in the oven?" she asked.

What Cassie wanted most was to escape up the stairs with the bag so she could read the notebook Mrs. Dexter had given her, but she also didn't want anything to seem unusual. "Sure," she said. She followed her mother into the kitchen and plopped a big spoonful of the filling into a bowl.

"Did you find any good rocks?" her mom asked.

"Some nice quartzite. I gave a piece of it to Ben. And a few fossils and some flint. I was hoping for some agate or geodes, but I guess that's not the place for them."

"I was surprised that Kevin went," her mother remarked. "I never knew he liked rock hunting. I thought he was more into hunting deer."

"He is, Mom, but Jordan wanted to go really bad and he said he'd take us. Maybe he liked it. He found a pretty nice fossil. He says he's going to give it to his girlfriend. I'd like to be around to see that happen." Cassie grinned. She didn't know Melissa very well, but she was pretty sure that girl would not be impressed by a fossil shell. Better to give her a make-up case or something.

"How long 'til dinner?" she asked. "I need to get cleaned up and check my email." She turned away and bit her lip. Yeah, she did, but she sure wasn't looking forward to it.

"At least an hour. Go ahead. I don't need any help in the kitchen today. You'll get your turn tomorrow. You can always fall back on Hamburger Helper." Her mom grinned, teasing.

Cassie made a face. She liked to cook and didn't mind her regular Monday night supper duty. She sure wasn't going to use Hamburger Helper! Maybe a nice hot chicken curry.

As she headed for the stairs, her mom called after her, "By the way, if you don't have any after-school activities tomorrow, I'd like to pick you up and take you out to Whispering Springs so you can see how your room looks with the new lighting. I'm trying to get decorating ideas all planned. We don't have to stay long, but that way I can get more done during the rest of the week."

Cassie nearly stumbled on the stairs. Go to Whispering Springs again tomorrow? Already? Where would Ben be? She had counted on not going out there until at least next weekend. She cleared her throat, hoping she sounded enthusiastic. "Great, Mom. Sure, I can go. What about Ben?"

"I made arrangements for him to stay at Matt's house. He's been wanting to spend more time with him and they had such a good afternoon together today they begged to get together after school tomorrow."

She wasn't going to be able to watch him anyhow. She'd just have to hope that the Spy would be watching her and not her brother tomorrow afternoon.

After a quick shower, Cassie fished Mrs. Dexter's notebook out of the rock bag. Her heart beat faster. Was she about to find out the answers to some of her questions? Here it was, the story of another fourteen-year-old girl who had known the ghost. She ran her fingers over the writing on the cover, tracing the letters written by Mrs. Dexter when she was a teenager.

Secret. Keep Out.

Property of Felicity Graham

So that was her maiden name.
Cassie opened the cover and began to read.

May 31, 1955. For a week Winona has been hearing a voice. They call her place Whispering Springs because something sounds like whispering out there, but no one heard any real words. Until Winnie's 14th birthday a week ago, that is. Right after they had her birthday cake. Winnie heard "Happy Birthday" coming out of thin air. She thought she was crazy.

It wasn't long before the voice was saying, "Help me." She didn't know who wanted her help or what kind of help, and she was scared, so she tried not to pay any attention.

It didn't work. The voice wouldn't leave her alone. Today Winnie told me that it's the ghost of her grandmother's cousin, Annie Gwynne. Annie has been dead a long, long time. Fifty-eight years! She died when she was only 14, like us. She has the same birthday as Winnie. I guess that's why she started talking to Winnie on her birthday.

June 2, 1955. Annie is talking more and more. Can you imagine a voice coming out of nowhere, no body, no face? Annie wants Winnie to find a letter, but Winnie doesn't know what she is talking about. Today Winnie fainted when we were together up in her room. When she came to, I asked her why and she said, "I think Annie touched me. It was like being smothered with ice."

June 14, 1955. Winnie saw the ghost today. Just a shadow of it. A dark-haired girl in a blue dress. She beckoned Winnie to follow her. Winnie tried but her father made her do some chores. He wouldn't listen to a thing Winnie said about the ghost. "Get that nonsense out of your head, girl," he hollered. "Work will set you right." He made Winnie do double chores to keep her from thinking foolish thoughts.

June 19, 1955. Annie begs Winnie to talk to her, read to her, find her letter. Winnie doesn't dare let on that she hears Annie any more. She sure can't tell anyone else that she sees her, either. Her parents think she is losing her mind. They talk about sending her away to a boarding school. Her dad even locks her in the cellar, saying that will cure her.

Cassie understood how Winona felt. At least now she knew for sure she wasn't imagining Annie. Poor Winona! Cassie hoped she wouldn't have the same problems with her own family.

Cassie had thought it would help to find out more about another girl who had seen and heard Annie, but it didn't. Instead, it made the whole thing seem more real. If Annie was still there, all these years after Winnie saw her, over a hundred years after she died, would she ever go away? She could imagine how frightened Winnie felt when her father thought she was going crazy and would lock her in the cellar or double her chores, or threaten to send her away. He even had the priest lecturing her not to tell lies. She had no one to turn to but Felicity. Like me, she thought. I only have Jordan.

Cassie finished the notebook and read the letters from Winona Cranston, who was now Mrs. Winona Miller. Winnie and Felicity never did figure out why Annie was there or how to help her. Gradually, as Winnie grew up, Annie left her alone except for a birthday greeting or occasionally whispering her name. It was as if Annie knew that Winnie couldn't help her, or maybe she knew what torment her ghostly communication caused. Winnie said Annie grew sad and just withdrew.

Mrs. Miller still mentioned Annie in her letters from Minnesota. She wondered what had become of her, whether she ever found what she was looking for. When Mrs. Miller came back after her father died, she went through the house, not knowing whether she hoped she would find Annie or not. She didn't, not really. She took only a few things from the house, just closed it up and left it with its unhappy memories. She didn't even tell anyone she had been there. Her father's funeral was private and his ashes were scattered on the land. When Winona

Miller left, she said, "Goodbye, Annie," and she thought she heard a sob. That was all.

What good would it do to write to Winona Miller? If she hadn't figured it out in all these years, how was she going to help Cassie? But Cassie had to try. Felicity must not have known every detail, couldn't have written down everything.

Cassie turned on her computer. She was so tired. Her grandmother said when you were in an emergency or something that really stressed you out, you'd be fine for awhile, going on adrenaline, but then you'd crash. How did she put it, "Too many withdrawals from the energy bank." Yeah, thought Cassie. My account is bankrupt.

She could hardly keep her eyes on the screen as it booted up and she signed on. She ignored the new messages and keyed in a note.

Dear Mrs. Miller,

You don't know me, but my family is buying your old home at Whispering Springs out on Mill Creek. I started hearing a voice. Then I saw some kind of illusion of the past and felt cold. I found out from Mrs. Felicity Dexter that things like that happened to you when you were my age. I am 14 and was born on May 24th. I think the same ghost is communicating with me now and I don't know what to do. Can you help me?

Thank you,
Cassie Wade, Topeka, Kansas

She clicked on Send. There, she did it. She sighed heavily. Would Winona Miller be able to help, or would she even want to discuss it?

Cassie almost got up and went downstairs without looking at the messages she received but she finally worked up the courage to check them. She hoped there wouldn't be one from the Spy, but there it was. No subject, but by now she knew the email address. She put her head in her hands for a minute. She sure wasn't sleepy any longer. She took a deep breath. Okay, Mister Spy, she thought, here I come. She opened the message. It said,

No more stupid tricks. Don't think that what happened out there today will discourage me. You'd better start thinking seriously about what I can do to you and your brother. At least you showed up. For that I'll give you another chance. Just one. Work fast if you know what's good for you.

No use trying to explain to him that she hadn't caused the wind or howling in the graveyard. No use trying to explain that her parents didn't know about any treasure. No use telling him that people had looked for that treasure for years and that Annie's ghost wanted a letter, too, but no one had found either of them. They probably didn't exist. No use telling him that if there was a treasure, the ghost was probably protecting it from both of them. She rubbed her neck, remembering his hands on it.

But maybe Ben's life and hers depended upon her finding something no one had found in over a hundred years!

I'm Here

It was hard to concentrate in school the next day. Cassie kept remembering that awful email. "You'd better start thinking seriously about what I can do to you and your brother."

What kind of a man would threaten kids like that? For what? A treasure that wasn't his? Why hadn't he bought the old place himself? Then he could have looked for it all he wanted and it would have been his when he found it. Maybe he didn't have the money to buy it, even for back taxes, whatever that cost. Or maybe he had learned about the treasure too late and her family had already contracted to buy Whispering Springs.

A thought struck her. He must be the man who stole the photograph from Miss Mossman and called to tell her she had to "cooperate." But if that was true, he would have the letter that was on the back of it. It must not have told him what he wanted to know. Was that the letter Annie's ghost wanted so badly? Maybe Miss Mossman was in as much danger as Cassie thought she and Ben were in.

All day Cassie dreaded hearing the last bell.

After school she'd be on the way to Whispering Springs. Would the Spy be there? Even during art class while she was finishing her mosaic she could hardly keep her mind on it.

"Hey, Cas," Jordan hollered as they were leaving school. "Are you walking home with me?"

"Not today," Cassie answered. She bit her lip. "Mom is taking me out to Whispering Springs to work on decorating ideas."

Jordan sidled up and gave Cassie a big hug. "Be careful," she whispered. "Stay focused. Maybe you'll learn something that will help."

"Yeah, okay. I'll try," Cassie mumbled. She squared her shoulders.

On the way to Whispering Springs, Cassie's mother chattered happily about her decorating plans, how pleased she was that they didn't have to rip out the plaster in all of the rooms, how much faster it was coming along than she had expected. She was so engrossed that she scarcely noticed that Cassie was quieter than usual.

Good thing, thought Cassie, or she'd be grilling me on what's wrong.

At the house, Cassie's mom showed her wall-paper samples and paint swatches. She led Cassie through room after room pointing out old furnishings she planned to save and where she wanted to put special antiques from her mother's family, and how the furniture from their little house in Topeka would fit in.

Cassie did her best to pay attention and act interested. It was a shame. Ordinarily she would love to be this involved with decorating plans. Sometimes she thought she wanted to study interior decorating as a career. This was a perfect opportunity to be a part of restoring and decorating a grand old house but her mind was elsewhere.

Even in her room, where they decided on a mauve, cream and light green color scheme, colors Cassie loved, it was hard to imagine it all really happening. How could it, with Annie and the Spy lurking to spoil everything?

Where were they now? Watching everything?

Her mother turned on the new track lighting and showed Cassie how it worked. "I loved the idea, so I had track lighting put in the room I'm using for a studio, too," she said. "Won't it be wonderful, each of us with our own art studio?" she said, breathless with excitement. "I can't tell you how many years I've dreamed of this and saved for it."

Cassie couldn't think what to say except, "Thanks, Mom." She gave her a big hug. She wished she felt as excited about it as her mother did. She wished she could add, "I can't wait to move in here," but it choked in her throat.

"Oh, and Cassie, I've discovered the most wonderful four poster bed behind all that junk in the cellar. It's just gorgeous and in really good condition. It would be perfect in your room. If you'd like it, that is."

The four poster. Was it the one Annie showed

her with the illusion that first day? Annie's bed? She nearly gasped. Could she sleep in Annie's bed? She could say no, surely she could. She wanted to, but instead she found herself saying, "I'd love it, Mom."

Her mother noticed the tins of letters on the walnut desk. "Dad told me you'd found some old letters and brought them up here," she said. "Anything interesting?"

"I haven't read these yet," Cassie answered. "I took one tin home and read the letters in it. I found out some things about the Gwynnes. Joseph Gwynne's wife was named Adele. She had a sister in Nebraska. Adele's baby, Johnnie, died of the croup when he was only two years old."

"Dying young wasn't unusual in those days," her mother replied. "We're lucky to have better medical care now. You know, those old letters might make an interesting school project. I'll bet the historical museum would love to have them, afterwards."

"Dad said I could have anything I want from the cellar. He thinks it's a lot of old junk," Cassie said.

"Most of it probably is, but there's no telling what kind of interesting· historical information might be hidden in the mess. If it intrigues you, go ahead and look."

Her mom said she needed to go down and do some measuring in the kitchen and pantry, and after that she wanted to finish removing wallpaper in the dining room before they went home. Cassie asked if she needed some help. Her mother laughed. "With all the work this place needs, I always need help, but not with what I'm doing today. I'll put you to work another time. You haven't had a chance to explore since we've made all these improvements. Maybe you'd like to just take some time and look around. If that gets boring, you can read your letters or haul some more stuff from the cellar to the barn. We have real lighting down there now." She headed down the stairs.

This was her chance! Her first chance, anyway. Who knew how many times she would have to look to find what the Spy and Annie were looking for, if it was even the same thing.

She decided right away not to spend her time at the house reading those letters. She could take them home and read them. It was more important to see what else she could find. She looked around her room with keen attention now. Was it going to be like something out of Nancy Drew where there was a hidden compartment somewhere? Good luck finding one in this house. You could spend a year going over the walls and still miss it. Or maybe there had been one in a fancy piece of furniture that might not even be in the house any more.

Cassie touched the painted-over writing on the door post. Now she knew what it said, at least partly. "Annie Gwynne, May 24, 18??" Annie must have carved it on one of her birthdays, but which one? She only lived to be fourteen, Cassie reminded herself.

"I don't remember the lightning strike. They say I was killed instantly," came a whisper from across the room.

Cassie let out a little cry.

Sitting at the desk was the merest wisp of a girl, transparent. She was wavering as though she were about to disappear.

"Annie," Cassie whispered back, her knees weak. "Are you here with me, or is it my imagination?"

"I'm here," the ghost replied. "I'm always here."

Annie's Story

assie stayed very still, afraid to move, afraid she really *was* hallucinating, even afraid that if she didn't react just right to Annie, she would go away. *Isn't that what I want?* She was surprised that the answer was no. She wanted to know Annie and everything about her. How could this wispy girl hurt anyone? Yet, she had protected Cassie from the Spy out there in the cemetery.

"Are you haunting me because I'm fourteen, like you?" she managed to ask.

"Is that what you call it, haunting?" Annie asked. "I've been trying for all these years to find someone to help me. I thought Winona could, but she couldn't. I hoped maybe with your family it would be different. I've tried to talk to everyone who ever came here, but only you and Winona could ever hear me. Maybe it is because we have the same birthday and are fourteen."

Annie seemed to grow even dimmer, like a faint light that was fading away.

"What's happening to you?" Cassie asked.

"I think it's hard for you to see me for long until

you are used to me and really believe I'm here. It's hard for me to be visible in the daylight, too. It would be easier if you had something of mine to connect us."

"Like your iris pin?" Cassie asked.

"You found it?" Annie asked, obviously pleased.

"My little brother did. He gave it to me. It's beautiful, Annie," Cassie said.

"Oh, please, bring it with you. Wear it. That will help a lot," Annie said. "I would be so happy to see something from my mother after all these years." She let out a soft sob.

"What's wrong?" Cassie took a cautious step toward Annie.

" I miss my mother so much. It was hard living alone with my father after she died. He loved my mother more than anything in the world. When she died, he took all the photographs of her away. I don't know whether he just hid them or destroyed them. I used to try to find them when he was out of the house, but I never did.

"I begged him to let me have just one picture of my mother to keep, to remember her by, but he wouldn't. He said my face was reminder enough to him of what he had done to her and how he had lost her and Johnnie. When I cried because I thought he couldn't bear to look at me, he would hug me and tell me how much he loved me, that I was all he had left but that it was hard for him. He never seemed to see that it was hard for me, too.

"I tried to get Winona to help me find a photo. Surely my father must have kept at least one somewhere. And the letter she left for me. When she was dying, she called me into her room alone and told me that there was a secret that I would learn someday. She didn't want to tell me when I was ten years old, but she said she wrote a letter for me, to explain, and hid it. She wouldn't tell me where it was. She told me she had left a clue for me that I would figure out when I was older, but I died before I ever did.

"Mother told me that if I ever needed anything, I should ask her sister Marie in Nebraska. I only saw Aunt Marie once, but she wrote us letters."

"I read some of the letters from your Aunt Marie," broke in Cassie. "She wanted you and your mother to come to visit her."

"Yes!" said Annie. "And we did go one summer. I liked her so much. That's why I wanted to go and live with her when I was older, when it was so lonely with my father.

"I used to go out to my mother's grave and talk to her, remember our lives before she died. I missed her so much! My father missed her, too, but instead of us growing closer after she died, he kept more and more to himself. He had angry days and sad ones; he never smiled. He didn't like me to go away from the ranch to visit anyone, and he didn't want anyone to come here. The only time I saw anyone was at church or school."

Cassie tried to imagine what it must have been

like to live here alone with a father like that. What would she do without a friend like Jordan?

"He made me go to church," Annie went on. "He said at least my mother and Johnnie were in Heaven, a place he never expected to see. He wouldn't tell me why. He was angry when I asked him why he thought he would go to Hell, shouting to me that Greed is a deadly sin and I should remember that. He really frightened me. I started wondering if greed had something to do with the secret my mother had written about and I almost went crazy not knowing."

"But how could it?" asked Cassie.

"I don't know. I hoped my mother's letter would explain. When I was almost fourteen, he started talking about how a proper young lady should go to a finishing school and learn how to conduct herself in society, especially a girl with 'prospects,' and he wanted me to find the right husband to take care of me and the ranch when he was gone. I didn't know whether to be scared or glad he was planning to send me away. The ranch was all I had ever known. I wrote to my Aunt Marie and asked her what I should do about boarding school and I told her how much I wanted a picture of my mother."

Cassie hoped with all her heart that Annie would tell her that Aunt Marie helped her, but knowing that Annie was still here, dead at fourteen, she knew that hope was futile.

Annie went on, "Aunt Marie wrote back to me

and invited me to come to live with her family and go to school with my younger cousin, Dora. It sounded wonderful, to be a part of a family again. It was just want I wanted! She said she had a letter for me from my mother, something my mother had asked her to save for me and give to me when I was older. I was so excited and curious. Maybe it was the letter my mother told me about."

Cassie's knees gave way. She sank slowly to the floor and sat cross-legged with her back against the wall, listening. If Adele sent the letter to Marie, it probably wasn't here. She was never going to find it for the Spy!

"Best of all, Aunt Marie sent a picture with her letter to me. It was my parents' wedding photo. My mother looked beautiful and my father was young and handsome. It was the most precious gift she could have given me, and it came on my fourteenth birthday. It made that day the happiest one I could remember since before my mother died. I read her letter over and over. I looked at myself in the mirror and compared my face to my mother's. Did I look like her? I kept all this a secret for three weeks, but I was so cheerful that my father started asking me what had happened. He did not approve."

"But why not?" Cassie asked. "Wasn't he glad to see you happy again?"

"I think he was afraid of losing me if I got over my grief but I didn't understand that then. I showed him the letter and the photo. I don't know why I thought he would be pleased about it, too. It was during a big thunderstorm and we were stuck in the house. It seemed like the kind of day that would be happier with something to look forward to and memories to treasure. At least that's what I thought, but I didn't know my father well enough.

"He went on a rampage, screaming at me that I was determined to torture him with memories and leave him alone forever by running off to Nebraska. He tore up my aunt's letter and threw the pieces all over the dining room, shouting that I would never hear from her again. He said she was lying about a letter from my mother. Worst of all, he threw their wedding photo into the fireplace. There was no fire in it, and that seemed to make him even angrier. He fished it out and held it over a candle until it started to burn.

"That's when I ran. I couldn't bear it. I couldn't bear to see my father like that, to lose the only picture I'd seen of my mother in four years. I was going to run to her grave and cry there, even though it was during a storm. I never made it. I got scared of the lightning and ran under a big cottonwood tree. I knew people weren't supposed to be under trees in a thunderstorm, but I didn't care. It looked like shelter to me. I was so hurt and lonely and desperate I wasn't even thinking."

"Oh, Annie," whispered Cassie, "That's when the lightning struck."

115

Now I Have You

Annie's voice was so quiet, so soft. Cassie had to strain to hear her. There was silence for a moment. Please, Cassie wanted to say, don't fade away now. Don't stop. Tell me your story. She wanted desperately to know.

"After the lightning hit, I came back. I wandered around the house, the graveyard and the springs, hoping to find my mother or Johnnie. Wouldn't they be ghosts, too? But I never did.

"I tried to search for my mother's letter but I never found it. For forty-three years until my father died, I tried to talk to him, to tell him I loved him. He was such an unhappy old man. But he could never hear more than a whispering sound. He would stop what he was doing and listen, as though he were trying to make out my words, but I could never make him understand.

"That's the worst part of being a ghost, the loneliness. Being able to see and hear people, but no one could see or hear me. Days seemed like an eternity.

"And to be here, but not here. To be able to watch the world but not be a part of it. Gradually I learned to focus what was left of me into my hands or my voice, or to gather the weak breeze into something stronger, but still no one noticed me. I could only focus like that for a short time and it was hard to do. It made me so tired."

Cassie considered how it would be, to be invisible like that, ignored, alone. She looked at her hands. What if she couldn't draw, couldn't paint any more? She shuddered.

"After my father died and his brother's grandson Adam Cranston inherited our house, I tried to talk to him and his wife. It was always the same. They only heard whispering sounds. But listening to the Cranstons, I began to learn strange things about my family. The Cranstons were very upset about people sneaking out here looking for a treasure that was supposed to be hidden on our land, or maybe in the house, or even in the cemetery. There were rumors about my father being very rich and no one knowing how he got all that money, or where he kept it. I'd never heard anything like that before.

"Adam didn't believe the stories. He insisted that people made up a lot of nonsense because my father was such a strange old hermit after I died. Sarah argued that my father had to have gotten a lot of money somewhere when he was young and if he hadn't spent it all, where was it? Then Adam would get annoyed and say that if there was a fortune, it was likely all spent many years ago. If it hadn't been, why hadn't any of it been in my father's bank account when he died? And Sarah would say maybe the diggers were right, that it was buried out here somewhere. Adam would blow up and say, 'Why don't you get a shovel and go dig for it yourself?'

"Until then, I never knew there was a mystery, except why my father blamed himself for my mother's and Johnnie's deaths. Now I wanted to know whether my father really was rich, whether there was a treasure, and how he got all that money."

"That's the treasure the man wants, the one who was in the cemetery," Cassie said. "Is it real? Was that you who scared him into letting me go?"

"It was the only way I could protect you. He's dangerous. He's been skulking around out here for a couple of weeks now. I don't know if the treasure is real, but he believes it is. I tried to warn you about him the first day you were here."

"So it was you who screamed in the kitchen and slammed the door to keep me and Ben out of the house?"

"Yes. I didn't know how else to warn you. I didn't know you would be the first person to really hear me since Winona."

"I heard about Winona from her friend Felicity, Mrs. Dexter," said Cassie. "Her granddaughter Jordan is my best friend. Tell me about what happened between you and Winona." Maybe it would help to hear how Annie remembered it.

"When the Cranston's daughter Winona was

born on my birthday, I thought it was a sign. She would be able to see me someday. I stayed close to her most of the time. I loved having a family in the house, having a child around. They never saw me, but I played among them, with them. I watched everything they did. I sang to Winona when she was going to sleep.

"When she was fourteen, they had a big birthday party. I was so happy for her. When it was over, she was sitting in her room, this one, and I told her happy birthday. She looked around with a start. Could she really have heard me? I said, 'Hello, Winona.' She whirled around, looking for where my voice came from. She couldn't see me, but I was dancing with delight. After all these years, someone could hear me! I couldn't stop talking to her. Can you imagine what it was like to have someone who could hear you after fifty-eight years?

"I hoped Winona could help me find out the truth about my family. Maybe she could find the letter my mother hid for me. Or maybe she could find out what happened to the one my mother sent to Aunt Marie. I worked hard to get Winona to believe in me. She could see me, a little. I didn't understand why my touch was so cold to her. But, to have a friend, someone to talk to, was beyond joy.

"What I hadn't counted on was her family. Her parents thought she was going crazy. Her father punished her for lying and thinking foolish thoughts by doubling her chores. Then he threatened to send her away to a boarding school. I couldn't stand the thought of that, losing my only friend, my cousin.

"At first, I pushed her to help me find the letter, but as things got worse with her father, Winnie tried not to talk about me or let them know she could still hear and see me. I knew I had to leave her alone. It was the hardest thing I ever did, letting Winnie go. Watching her, loving her, without being able to talk with her any more. It got easier after awhile to go back to the shadows and be alone again."

Annie had been staring out the window as she spoke. Now she looked directly at Cassie. "And now I have you," she said. "Will you be my friend? Will you help me? Oh, please, don't let it be like it was with Winnie."

Campbell

assie hesitated. Friends with a ghost? Was that possible? Could she trust Annie? She thought of all the times she had been frightened by her, though she wasn't frightening now.

"I'm trying to help you, too," Annie offered.

"But what can I do?" Cassie said. "That man -- I call him the Spy -- says he will hurt my little brother Ben if I don't cooperate with him and help him find the treasure. You saw what he did in the graveyard. He thinks there are some kind of directions, or a clue, or maybe a map or something, in a letter I'm supposed to look for. He said I'd better work fast. I don't know how much time I have before he does something desperate. I think he's the same one who threatened my neighbor, Miss Mossman."

"Why would he threaten her?" Annie asked. Cassie's apparent acceptance of her friendship seemed to make Annie grow a little stronger. She didn't look quite so faint and unclear now.

Cassie grew excited as she realized Annie might be able to help with the puzzle. "Miss Mossman is ninety years old. A couple of weeks ago, her niece in Nebraska sent her an old trunk that used to be her mother's. In it, she found a photo of Whispering Springs! And fastened to the back was a letter addressed to 'Annie.'"

"My letter!" Annie gasped. "Oh, Cassie, bring me my letter. How could it be in your neighbor's mother's things?"

"I'm sorry, Annie," Cassie said sadly, "I can't bring you the letter. Someone stole it. Some workmen were in Miss Mossman's house doing repairs right after she found it and then it was gone. Someone called her and asked her a lot of questions about this house. He threatened her, too, but she doesn't know anything."

Annie looked as though she were trying hard to put together the pieces of a puzzle that was a hundred years old. "So, Miss Mossman's mother had it. And she was from Nebraska. What was her name?"

"I don't know," Cassie answered. "But I can ask her. Why?"

Annie looked hopeful. "I have the strangest feeling that she is related to my Aunt Marie," she said. "Maybe I still have some family after all, not just my cousin Winona, who is so far away."

"I'll find out and tell you next time I come. But that man must have the photo and the letter. I don't know if we'll ever get it from him. If that letter did tell about the treasure, he'd have found it by now, so I don't think it does. There must be another one."

"But Cassie, just to have any letter from my mother, after all these years, to read what she wrote to me before she died . . . Don't you see, even if it doesn't tell me about the treasure, it's a treasure to me."

Cassie did see, but how could she get it from the Spy? She realized that if she found another letter, one Annie's mother hid at Whispering Springs, it probably was the one with the clue the man wanted so badly. She ran a hand through her hair and sighed. Annie wouldn't want him to have it. She was sure of that.

"His name is Jason Campbell," Annie blurted out. "I've been watching him the whole time he's been here. It must be the same man, don't you think? No one else has been sneaking around out here. He lurks around with something that must be a camera, but it doesn't look like the kind we had. It's so small. He has something he talks into. It fits in his pocket. I can't figure out how it works. It doesn't even have any wires. Why would anyone talk to something like that?"

"He must have a cell phone," Cassie said. "And a digital camera. So that's how he got that photo of me on the porch."

"A what?" Annie asked.

"I'll explain another time. I don't know how much time I have before my mother wonders what I'm doing up here, or wants to head home. We have to think about what to do next."

"Take the boxes of letters with you," Annie said. "If you don't, Mr. Campbell might get them first. I don't want him to have them. I don't think he noticed them in the basement. He was down there lots of times shoving stuff around looking for something, maybe a secret cabinet or a treasure chest. Who knows? They were under so much stuff he never paid any attention to them. I don't think my mother's letter is in them, though. They are all letters to her. Unless she hid hers in one of them."

"Okay," said Cassie. "I'll take them home and see what I can find. But if the letter we need isn't with them, what then? And what about the treasure?"

"Then we have to look where no one has thought of looking in all these years."

"Where could that be?" Cassie asked. "I thought lots of people had searched all over the house and land."

"But they didn't find anything, did they? So there must be someplace they didn't think to look."

"If there is a treasure," Cassie reminded her.

"If there's not, I want to know. And I still want my mother's letter. No matter what. Oh, Cassie, will you mind so much having me around, haunting you, as you called it?"

"I don't think so. Not now that I know you aren't trying to harm me, that we can be friends. But it is going to be hard to keep other people from thinking something weird is going on, that I'm not hallucinating or something."

"Yes, but I'm not the only one causing that problem. There's Jason Campbell," Annie pointed out. She was staring out the window again. "It's so pretty at this time of year. I always loved spring. There are many more redbuds now, more trees. There were hardly any trees when I was alive." She jumped, startled. "There he is, watching the house!"

Cassie sprang to her feet and looked out the window. "Where?" she asked.

"In the lilac bushes." Annie pointed.

Cassie could only make out a slight movement. Campbell must be wearing camouflage clothing, like a hunter might, she thought. Usually anything to do with the Spy -- Campbell, she corrected herself -- made her fearful, but now she was just angry. Who was he anyway to think he could get away with it? She and Annie were going to stop him!

She hoped.

A Chest in the Coal Bin

Cassie wished she had some way to get rid of Campbell right now. If she went to the police or the sheriff and told what he had done to her, and showed them the sympathy cards and the email, maybe they would arrest him and try him for something. But how could she prove they came from him? His name wasn't on anything.

How could she even identify him? The only time she had seen his face was in the tower room window that first day, and the short glimpse she got wasn't enough that she could recognize him. All she knew was that he had a beard. If she did go to the authorities and named him, he'd probably explain it all away and then he'd truly be ready to do her and Ben some harm. And maybe Miss Mossman, too. No, she and Annie would have to beat him at his own game. But how?

Annie floated toward the door. "Let's see what else you could take home from the cellar," she said. "If he's watching, at least he'll know you are looking for what he wants."

It wasn't much of a plan, but it gave her a place

to begin. Cassie started down the stairs. It wasn't really spooky to have Annie's ghost following her. By now, Annie's shadowy presence almost seemed familiar, companionable in a strange way.

Cassie headed through the kitchen, opened the cellar door and flipped on the light switch.

"Oh, there you are," her mother called from the pantry next door. "If you're going to the cellar, would you take this box of tiles down there?" She stepped out and handed it to her.

Cassie nearly fell down the stairs when she saw Annie pass right through her mother's body. She gasped and grabbed the door frame. The box of tiles clattered to the floor, breaking several of them.

"Cassie, what's wrong?" her mother demanded.

She hadn't felt a thing, Cassie realized. She doesn't even know a ghost floated right through her. Cassie couldn't find her voice. She glanced down the stairs still hanging onto the door frame for support. Annie was at the bottom of the steps, only visible from the shoulders up.

"Cassie?" her mother asked. "What is it?"

She hadn't bargained on something like this. No wonder it had been so hard for Winona. She couldn't very well pretend nothing had happened but if she told her mother what had, there was no telling where she might end up, or what might happen to Ben and Miss Mossman. It was clear to her that Annie had no idea what it was like for someone to communicate with her when no one else knew she was there.

Cassie thought fast.

"I don't know mom. It was so quiet in the house. You startled me, that's all. I almost fell." Well, that was all true. She just left out the part about watching a ghost walk right through her mother.

"Too bad about those tiles but I'm glad you didn't fall and get hurt." Her mother picked up the pieces and handed Cassie the box. "You can still take them down if you're going. I'm about done here for the day. Maybe another ten minutes. I'll meet you at the car."

"Okay." Cassie let out her breath slowly and took the first deliberate step down the stairs.

In the cellar, she noticed some doors she hadn't seen the afternoon she had been carrying things to the barn. Now that there were lights down there, and a lot less junk, she looked around and discovered there were at least two other rooms. Annie seemed to be halfway through one of the doors.

"I was always scared of the coal bin when I was alive," Annie was saying. "It was so dark. It's in here."

"Annie, wait. Why did you go right through my mother?"

"She didn't know the difference. It doesn't hurt people. I found that out years ago. Only the ones who can hear or see me, like you and Winona, ever feel that I'm there. But I feel them. It's like a warm hug. It's like being real for just a second or so."

Cassie was speechless. Was she going to have to

watch Annie passing through her family members, looking for warmth? How was she ever going to watch that without reacting and having people think she was a mental case? Would Ben feel it? She was pretty sure her dad wouldn't.

"Annie, remember all the problems Winona had when her parents thought she was crazy?" Cassie began. "If you do things like that right in front of me, it's going to cause a lot of trouble. I nearly fell down the stairs, and I'm just lucky my mom believed what I told her. You have to be more careful around other people."

"I'll try," Annie said. "But I'm used to coming and going as I please after all these years. It's going to be hard."

Cassie found a place for the box of tiles and moved over to the door beside Annie. "Is it unlocked?" she asked.

"I think so. Why would anyone lock the door to a coal bin?" Annie asked.

"Sure you want to go in there?" Cassie wanted to know. "If it's that creepy?"

Annie smiled. "I thought it was when I was little. I know better now. I don't think Campbell has been in that room yet. He took one look and figured there wasn't anything valuable or useful in there. There weren't any lights down here then. Who would store something they cared about in an old coal bin?"

She laughed. "He's dangerous to you, but not to me. I walked right through him. He never knew I was there." She changed her tone to a very serious one. "But if I want to, I can concentrate myself and blast someone. It takes everything I have to do that. I can't do it often. It's very tiring."

"Do ghosts have to rest? Do they sleep?" Cassie asked. She had visions of Annie floating around her room all night even while she was asleep. She didn't want Annie watching her all the time. Not like she watched Winona.

"Not the way living people do," Annie said. "Sometimes I wish I did. Sometimes I just need to be quiet and let time pass."

"Annie, are there any other ghosts at Whispering Springs?" Cassie asked. She had to know.

"No, just me. Why would there be more?"

"My friend Jordan said there were stories that all of your family are ghosts and you're out here protecting the Gwynne treasure."

"I wish I did have my family with me. Then I could find out everything I need to know. I'd love to see my mother and Johnnie again. As I told you, after I died I looked for them. I thought they might be ghosts too. But I'm the only one and I'm not guarding anything. Except you. Come on, open the door."

Well, maybe that was some relief, that Annie was the only ghost. No one else was watching her. Except Campbell.

Cassie lifted the old latch. The door creaked open. The sound was eerie enough even without a ghost at her side. She tried to think how this would look in a movie. Spooky!

Annie was right about the coal bin. The room was black with coal dust. There wasn't any pile of coal left in it, though. It must have been left empty years ago when a new furnace was installed by the Cranstons and the old coal-burning stoves were removed. At least that's what her father said they had once used to heat the house.

What could Annie possibly hope to find in the coal bin? Surely she had plenty of time to look there in all the years since she died.

"It's behind the coal chute," Annie said, as if reading her thoughts.

The boards of the slanted coal chute were cracked and filthy with coal dust.

"There's something wedged behind it," Annie continued. "I've always wanted to know what it was."

Shoved behind the base of the chute was something with a sooty black cloth over it. It was partly covered by a few lumps of coal. Cassie pushed a corner of the fabric aside gingerly with one finger. Ugh. Not only was it saturated with coal dust, it was covered with cobwebs, too. Under the cloth was a small wooden chest. Cassie grimaced but cleared away the coal and pulled the box out.

Annie gave a strangled cry and sank down beside it. She touched it gently. "Oh, Johnnie," she whispered. "Did father hide your toys under the coal? Why didn't he give them away or bury them with you?" She pulled on the lid of the box but her touch had no effect. "Cassie, help me," she said.

Cassie was openmouthed. "You mean your father hid your little brother's toys in here?" she finally asked. "They've been here all these years?"

"I never saw them after he died," Annie replied. She tugged at the lid of the chest again. "Or maybe my mother hid them. Maybe my father wouldn't let her keep them . . . he wouldn't let me have a photo of her."

Cassie wasn't enthused about touching the grimy chest again but she carried it into the other room. She found a rag and wiped as much of the mess off of it as she could. She found a screwdriver and tried to pry the lid open. After several minutes of work, she finally succeeded in forcing it open.

Her eyes widened. Inside were a few antique toys. A wooden horse pull toy, a set of painted nesting boxes, some small wooden farm animals, a baby's ball sewn from velvet, and a small tin train engine. There were also a child's christening gown, a small boy's blue suit, and a photo of a dark-eyed little boy.

Annie snatched the photo. "Johnnie!" she exclaimed. "I didn't think I'd ever see a picture of you again!"

After a moment it slipped through her fingers and fell. She couldn't hold on any longer. Cassie picked up the photo and put it back into the chest, looking at Annie with concern.

Just then, Cassie's mother called from the top of the stairs, "Let's go, Cas. It's later than I thought. Come on up."

Cassie looked at Annie. "I have to go," she said. "What shall we do with Johnnie's things?"

"Take them with you. I don't want anyone else to find them. I couldn't bear it if that horrible Jason Campbell found them or someone threw them away."

Cassie found a musty old blanket and wrapped it around the chest. She carried it up to the back door. Her mom was waiting to lock up.

"I'll just be a minute," she said. She ran upstairs to get the tins of letters. It's going to be an interesting evening, she thought.

It was hard to leave Annie sitting on the cellar floor and not even say goodbye.

More Email

hat kind of a man wouldn't allow his wife to keep pictures or mementos of their baby son? What kind of a man would not allow his daughter to keep a picture of her mother? No matter how Cassie thought about it, it didn't make sense. It was cruel.

And Annie . . . if what she wanted most was her mother's letter, how would they handle Jason Campbell, who wanted the letter for himself? Cassie was sure Annie would not want him to have it, ever. If there actually was a treasure, whose was it? If Annie had lived, it would have been hers. Whose would it be now? If Winona Miller had kept the house and found it, it would be hers. What would she do if they found it? Was it really finders keepers, losers weepers as all those treasure hunters seemed to think? It couldn't be that simple!

IF they found it. If Jason Campbell didn't get it. How was she going to keep it from him and still protect Ben?

Cassie was mulling all this over as her mother chattered happily about the house. "Wouldn't you love to know what the Gwynnes were like?" she asked. "What kind of people would build such a gorgeous house out here? They obviously had both good taste and plenty of money. I wonder where they got it."

Me, too, thought Cassie. Not only where they got it, but where it is now.

The strain of trying to figure out how she was going to maneuver between Annie and Jason Campbell was driving her crazy. At first she thought Annie would help her, and maybe Annie intended to, but the more Cassie thought about it, the more she realized that what might be right for her and her family might not be what Annie would want. Then what?

"Tell me what you found in the basement," her mother said. "You wrapped it up so mysteriously."

"It's a little old chest I found in the coal bin. It's pretty nice. Oak, I think, but it's filthy. That's why I wrapped it up in that blanket. I didn't think you'd want coal dust and cobwebs all over the trunk. I'll clean it up at home."

"Anything in it?" her mother asked.

Cassie hesitated, surprised that her mother didn't ask what she had been doing hunting around the coal bin or why she wanted to take the chest home with her instead of just cleaning it up there.

"I had to pry it open with a screwdriver and I

was really surprised at what was inside. There are some very old baby toys, a christening dress, a little boy's suit and a picture of a small boy. Maybe the baby that died and is buried in the graveyard out by the spring. Johnnie."

"Hmmm," her mother murmured. "Why would anyone stuff something like that in a coal bin?"

"That's what I was wondering, too," Cassie said.

"What were you doing in the coal bin, anyway?" her mother inquired.

"I didn't notice the other doors in the cellar before so I was curious. I saw a lump behind the coal chute and decided to investigate," she said.

"No strange hallucinations today?" her mother went on.

So, there it was. Her mother was still worrying about her. Clearly she hoped this trip hadn't produced any new occurrences. Maybe that's why she really brought her out here. To test her.

"Not hallucinations, Mom," said Cassie firmly. "They've never been hallucinations. There IS something strange in this house. Maybe no one else can feel it, but I can. Don't worry, though, Mom. I can handle it. It's no big deal." Right, she thought. Just the biggest deal of my life.

"But that man is still sneaking around here spying on us. Dad doesn't believe me. He said he would look to see if there was any evidence of him, but I don't think he has. I saw the man in the bushes watching the house again today."

Her mother's eyes narrowed. "Are you sure, Cassie? What would he want around here?"

"Yes, Mom, I'm sure," Cassie said, hoping she could convince her mother without telling her any more than that. "Jordan's grandmother says there was a rumor that the Gwynnes hid a treasure on the property. No one ever found it. Maybe he's looking for that."

"Oh, that old story." Her mother laughed. "I don't think there's much chance of that. People had plenty of time to look for it all these years. If there ever was one, it's long gone."

"I didn't know you knew about the treasure," Cassie replied, surprised.

"I'd forgotten all about that part of the legend until you mentioned it. I heard something about it when I was a kid and they were telling the stories about the whispering voices. Everyone knew it was just an old legend. I can't imagine that anyone would take it seriously."

"But what if HE does?" Cassie persisted.

"He'll get discouraged soon enough," her mother said. "But if it will make you feel better, I can ask the sheriff to check around."

Would that work? Would Campbell think that she had told someone about him, or just that her parents had decided to check to make sure he was gone? After all, he knew from the note her mother had left him in the barn that they were aware he had been there. With any luck, maybe a visit from the sheriff would scare him off. She could hope, but she didn't really believe it would work. Not for a man who said he would stop at nothing.

By the time they got home, Cassie's stomach felt like it was tied in knots. At least she had plenty to do. Tins of letters to read. A chest to clean and examine. Dinner to make. Homework. Email to check. That was the one she really dreaded. Jason Campbell knew she had been to the house today. He would want to know what she had found. And Winona Miller. What might she have to say? Cassie felt like some small insect caught in a web but she squared her shoulders. She had to be strong.

Dinner turned out great. Instead of curry, she made a spicy dish with chicken and cashews, one of her favorites, with rice and a fruit salad to cool everyone down.

She knew she'd have time during the next couple of days to read the letters and clean Johnnie's chest but her homework was due tomorrow, so she settled on doing that first. It was hard to concentrate knowing that she might find something important in her email, but she forced herself to do her geometry and put some finishing touches on the cathedral. School work seemed almost irrelevant now with a ghost and someone who was probably a criminal making her life so complicated.

She dreaded pressing the button on her Mac, but after meeting Annie in person this afternoon, something had changed. Scared or not, she couldn't just let things happen to her.

There were messages from both Winona Miller and Campbell. She chose Winona's first.

Dear Cassie,

It was quite a surprise to hear from you. I never thought anyone would see or hear Annie but me. I'm sorry you have to deal with this in your new home. I hope you won't be as unhappy there as I was. Annie never deliberately harmed me, but she did make my life miserable. She was so starved for a friend that she wouldn't leave me alone. I could never be without her. She wanted to be a part of everything I did, and she didn't want me to spend time with anyone else. She was an invisible presence, watching me every minute of the day and night. She pestered me to help her find a letter from her mother. I tried, but I couldn't find it.

My parents thought I was crazy. They'd catch me talking to someone who wasn't there. At least, she wasn't there for THEM. They'd find me doing things they didn't understand, like digging holes by the spring house or snooping around in the attic. My father meant well by his punishments and threats, but all he succeeded in doing was making my life more unbearable. There was no way I could convince my parents that Annie was real. Be very careful that the same thing doesn't happen to you!

Annie eventually realized that if she stayed with me continually and tried to make me do what she wanted, she would lose me completely because my parents would send me away, so she withdrew. She was still there. I could feel her watching, longing, waiting, but she didn't appear or talk to me often. It wasn't much better, knowing she was still there and how lonely she was. Can you see why I didn't want to come back to that house?

I wish I could help you, Cassie, but I can only give you a little advice. Be wary. Annie is friendly and helpful but she can be demanding and difficult, too. She doesn't mean to be, but she has been without friends or family for so long that she doesn't know how it feels to others. She never set out to hurt me, but she did just the same, and I'm worried that it will happen to you as well.

Good luck, Cassie. If it will help, tell me what happens. I don't know whether I'll be able to give you any advice that's useful, but I'll try.

Sincerely, Winona

So, her hunch that Annie might not be so easy to deal with was right. That was hardly reassuring. She wrote a quick note back to Winona to thank her and told her what had happened that day. She didn't bring up anything about Jason Campbell.

Now it was time to read his email. It was terse.

What did you take from the house today? Don't try to hide anything. Time is growing short. Don't waste it.

At least there weren't any new threats. She sent him a two-sentence answer.

I took two tins of letters from Nebraska and a small chest with baby toys in it. I haven't read the letters yet.

Whether he was in a hurry or not, he'd have to wait. Why was he in such a rush? Did he think her parents might find the treasure before he got his hands on it, or was there some other reason he needed it fast?

There was just enough time to call Jordan before going to bed.

Jordan was anxious to hear all about Cassie's experiences at Whispering Springs. "You actually SAW her?" she shrieked into the phone. "She talked to you, like in person? Oh, that is so cool."

"I'd like to see how cool you'd think it was if it were you Annie was talking to," Cassie said. It had seemed fine when she was talking with Annie in her room, but she also remembered the feeling of being smothered by Annie's attention later and nearly falling down the stairs when Annie passed through her mother.

"It's not going to be easy, Jordan," she said. "Annie and the Spy want the same letter. Even if I find it they can't both have it. Unless we can figure out a way to keep Ben and Miss Mossman safe without giving him the letter, how am I going to satisfy her? And who gets the treasure, if there is one?"

"Couldn't Annie's ghost scare the Spy away if she really wanted to?" Jordan asked.

"I'm not so sure. That man says nothing will stop him. He's desperate for some reason. What can she do to him anyway? Pushing him around in the cemetery rescued me, but it didn't make him leave."

Just before she went to bed, Cassie checked her email one more time. There was a new message from Campbell. It read,

Your neighbor doesn't seem inclined to be helpful. She insists she doesn't know anything. She's first on my list. Then your brother. Don't be stupid. You only have until Sunday. If you need any encouragement to get the job done, remember that I can get to them any time I like.

Get to them and do what? Did he mean to kidnap them?

Cousins

s soon as she got home from school the next day, Cassie got Johnnie's trunk out. She took everything out of it and cleaned it in the back yard where the soot could just wash off into the dirt under the bushes. It was a nasty job, but when she was done, the little chest looked nice. It was handmade and Johnnie's name was carved into the top of it. Cassie examined it carefully, hoping it might be like something out of a mystery book, with a secret compartment, but she didn't find anything like that.

The things inside it were in remarkably good shape after all those years. Cassie spread them out on her bed. Maybe she would find something among them she had missed in the cellar. Maybe even the letter Annie was looking for tucked in there somewhere. At first she was disappointed.

Then, on a whim, she took the nesting blocks apart to stack them, and to her surprise, something tied in a lacy handkerchief fell out. Cassie untied the fragile fabric and found a silver locket. The raised design was a lovely iris. An iris that exactly matched one of the irises in the bouquet on the brooch Ben found in the dirt. She opened the tiny catch and caught her breath. Inside were miniature photos of Annie and Johnnie. Annie must have been only about four years old and Johnnie looked a little younger than he did in the other photograph.

So Adele hid this. Irises again. Clearly she loved them. Now Cassie had two pieces of iris jewelry. There were irises on the front door and carved into the door frame. She remembered lots of irises coming up near the house, too. She fished the brooch out of her desk drawer. "Treasure the Irises," it said. Was that a clue? Was the treasure buried in the irises? If it was, how would she know where to look? It would take a long time to dig them all up. What would Jason Campbell say if she told him he had to dig them up to find the treasure? How could he do that without her parents knowing he was there?

He could tell her to do it, that's how, Cassie realized. Then she'd be in trouble with her parents. They wouldn't allow her to dig up all those irises just because she had a notion of finding a treasure under them.

Maybe she was jumping to conclusions. Maybe Adele just loved irises and the jewelry was the only treasure. She traced a finger over the iris design. It was so beautiful, but it wasn't giving up any more secrets tonight, and neither was Johnnie's chest. She carefully packed his belongings into it again and balanced it on a pile of books by her desk.

Time to read the letters. After reading for two hours she had learned more about Adele and Marie and their children, but she was disappointed that there was nothing like a helpful clue anywhere -- until she untied the last group of letters.

Dear Adele,
*   Your last letter worried me greatly. You sound so ill and frightened. Surely it cannot be that serious! What would happen to Joseph and Annie if you die? You mentioned sending me a photo and a letter to keep for Annie, and of course I would do that for you, my dear sister, but is it really necessary? Please do get well.*

But Adele hadn't gotten well, Cassie knew. That letter and photo must be the ones Campbell stole from Miss Mossman. Her grandmother had them. What was her family connection? Could her grandmother be Annie's Aunt Marie? What had Campbell learned from that letter?

Cassie phoned Miss Mossman and her words came out in a rush. "Miss Mossman, what were your mother's and your grandmother's names?"

"My mother's name was Dora and my grandmother's name was Marie. Dora Hall Mossman, and Marie Bowman Hall. Why?" she asked.

Even though Cassie half expected that answer,

she was still startled. It took her a moment to answer.

"Because now I know your family connection to the Cranston place," she said. "Your grandmother's older sister Adele came to Kansas to teach school and married Joseph Gwynne, the man who built the house. You were right that she died young. She died of pneumonia when she was only thirty-four, and before she died, she sent that photo and letter to your grandmother to keep for Annie. It has something to do with a secret that Annie was supposed to find out when she was older, but she never did because she died when she was only fourteen." Cassie paused to take a breath.

"Oh, my goodness," said Miss Mossman slowly. "What could have been in that letter? What kind of secret? Cassie, can you come over. I think we need to talk."

Cassie closed her eyes. Now she knew why Campbell thought Miss Mossman knew something about the house and the treasure. Now she knew why her neighbor might be in danger. What should she tell her?

For three years she had loved visiting Miss Mossman's house, playing duets with her on the piano, drawing, playing with her dozen cats. Never once had she worried about going over there, until now.

She gathered up the tins of letters. Miss Mossman might enjoy reading her grandmother's letters to her great-aunt in Kansas. She would learn a lot about her family from them. She stuffed the iris brooch into her jeans pocket and took the locket from Johnnie's chest, too. If she remembered what her mother had told her about family relationships, Annie and Johnnie were Miss Mossman's cousins.

Before she headed out the door, she scribbled a note and left it on the fridge, "I'm going to Miss Mossman's for a little while. I'll be back before dinner."

She didn't have to ring the doorbell at Miss Mossman's house. Her neighbor was waiting for her on the porch swing. Her eyes widened when she saw Cassie's armload of tin boxes.

"Cassie?" she said, lifting two of the boxes from the stack and opening the screen door. "What is all this you've brought?"

"Letters from your grandmother to Adele," Cassie answered. "I've read them. I thought you might like to read them, too."

They set the boxes down on the dining room table. Miss Mossman lifted one of the covers.

"Letters from the past," she murmured. "Cassie, I just can't quite believe that after all these years you have solved the riddle of that picture of the house and who the letter was for. What a strange coincidence that I would come to Kansas, too, and never know I had family here."

"But they were long dead, except for Joseph Gwynne," Cassie pointed out. "He didn't die until

1940 but he refused to have any contact with your family after his daughter Annie died in 1897."

They talked for a long time, Cassie talking as fast as she could, eager to tell Miss Mossman all she knew about Annie's family. Then came the question Cassie dreaded.

"But Cassie, why is this man who called me so interested in the old house? I can see now why he would think I might know something useful to him, but what is it he wants?"

Cassie took a deep breath. How was she going to explain to her neighbor, to warn her, without doing exactly what Jason Campbell had warned her not to do?

"Miss Mossman, he thinks Joseph Gwynne had a treasure and that it's still somewhere at Whispering Springs. He is desperate to get it. He thinks you can help him but just aren't cooperating. He might be dangerous."

"Yes, he might. But I can't help him and it doesn't look like I have any way to convince him of that, either," she said.

"Please be careful!" Cassie pleaded. "Maybe you should call the police."

"I will, if he threatens me again," promised Miss Mossman. "But I don't know his name so it's going to be hard for them to do anything."

Cassie hoped that would not be too late. She felt a weight in her chest. She knew his name, but she couldn't prove it. What would she do, say a ghost from 1897 told her who he was? She didn't dare tell, but what if keeping the secret made things even more dangerous for her friend? She couldn't tell. She just couldn't.

She pulled the brooch and locket out of her pocket. "Look," she said. "Ben found this when he was digging in the yard out there, and I found the locket in a little trunk in the cellar." She opened the locket and held it out. "Those are your cousins."

Miss Mossman took the jewelry and examined it closely. "I can see a family resemblance," she said. "Annie looks a lot like my mother did when she was small, with her light hair and lovely eyes. And Johnnie, well, he's so young, but that photo looks a lot like my brother at that age. How sad that they both died so young." She paused. "It's curious that both pieces of jewelry are irises, though. They look as though they were custom-made. That brooch is a very expensive gift to give a ten-year-old girl, but apparently the Gwynnes had plenty of money. My mother loved irises, too, just like my grandmother. She had a huge iris garden."

Maybe that's all it was, a family fascination with irises, thought Cassie. "But why would she have, 'Treasure the Irises' engraved on the brooch?" she asked. "Just because she loved those flowers?"

"Why not?" asked Miss Mossman. "Do you think it means something more?"

"I thought maybe the treasure, if there is one, or

was one, was buried in the irises," Cassie said. "But there are so many of them out there, how would anyone know where to look?"

Miss Mossman laughed. "It might be even harder, now, Cassie. Irises propagate themselves by sending out rhizomes underground. There are bound to be many more irises now than there ever were in Adele's day."

Cassie hadn't thought of that. "I wouldn't have to dig up ALL the irises. Maybe I could figure out about where the original flower beds were and concentrate on those." Annie might be able to help with that. But there was still no way she could think of to dig up the flowers without upsetting her parents. And how would she know how deep to dig?

"Ever thought of using a metal detector?" asked Miss Mossman. "If there were a treasure, and it contained coins or precious metals, that might work."

"I hadn't thought of that. It might work, but don't you think that man must have already tried it?" Cassie replied. Surely Campbell would have taken a metal detector all over the land out there if he was desperate to get his hands on a treasure. But maybe the treasure wasn't metal. What kind of treasure would that be? Paper money? Stock certificates? Jewels?

If there was a treasure, why should Jason Campbell get it? It wasn't his. But whose was it?

Annie's? She was dead, but Cassie bet Annie would think it was hers, just like the house. Winona's? But she had sold the house and its contents. Miss Mossman's? But the inheritance had gone to Joseph Gwynne's family when he died with no heirs. Ours? Until this moment, Cassie hadn't really considered that possibility. She had been too busy dealing with Annie and Campbell. But Campbell must think it would be theirs. She'd give anything to keep Ben and Miss Mossman safe, but if there was a real treasure, why should someone else have it?

Jealous

For a few days, things seemed almost ordinary. Cassie hadn't been out to Whispering Springs. That explained why she wasn't getting more email from Jason Campbell. He knew she hadn't done any more searching. Miss Mossman didn't mention any new threats. Cassie tried to stay occupied with everyday life but it was hard when Jordan kept asking whether anything had happened, and she still dreaded checking her email. Campbell had told her she had until Sunday. What would happen if she didn't find what he wanted by then?

On Thursday, her mother announced plans to spend the weekend working out at Whispering Springs. She had set up beds -- even had the four-poster ready for Cassie -- and there was a new stove and fridge already in the house. They were going out right after lunch on Saturday and would come home Sunday afternoon.

"And Cassie," her mother added, "This would be a perfect time to invite Jordan for that campout if you'd rather sleep outdoors. The weather is going to be great. Why don't you see if she can come?"

Cassie's heart seemed to flop over in her chest. A campout now? When Campbell would be watching and Annie expecting her to look for a letter? "But Mom," she started to protest, "Are you sure? Don't you need me to work on the house all weekend?" How else could she back out now and not have it look like something was wrong?

"It's fine, Cassie. We'll all be out there. I can spare you. You and Jordan will have a good time, I'm sure, and I know you won't see as much of each other after we move. I thought this was just what you wanted."

Cassie groped for another reasonable excuse. "But it's such short notice. I don't even know if her parents will let her go. We never mentioned it to them."

"Go ask," her mother said cheerily. "I don't think the Dexters have any big plans for this weekend."

Cassie half hoped Jordan's parents would say no, but they said it sounded exciting. Jordan danced around the living room singing the theme song from the Ghostbusters movie. Her parents didn't even raise an eyebrow. Apparently, they'd heard about the ghost rumors from her grandmother but they didn't take them seriously.

"We'll sleep out in the graveyard," Jordan said in a stage whisper. "It'll be s-o-o-o spooky! Maybe we'll even see a ghost. I can't wait."

"You and your ghost notions," said Mrs. Dexter with a laugh. "I don't believe in ghosts for a minute, but if you did see one -- or thought you did -- I don't think you'd be dancing around for joy like this. You'd run for the house."

"But Mom, the house is haunted, too. No escape there!" Jordan was her usual dramatic self.

Under her breath, Cassie said, "I thought you told me you weren't going to visit me there, ever, if there were ghosts howling all night long."

"Don't be silly, Cassie," Jordan replied. "I wouldn't miss this for anything. Even if they howl, and I bet they don't." She lowered her voice. "The only thing I'm worried about is Campbell. Let's hope he doesn't show up."

That evening, Cassie received another message from him. All it said was,

Time is running out.

First thing Saturday afternoon, Jordan demanded that Cassie show her the entire house, every room and closet, the cellar, the barn, and the paths to the spring and graveyard. Jordan acted as though she were collecting data for a report. The only place they hadn't been was the attic. Was she really going to write about it for the school newspaper? She'd better not. Cassie wasn't going to let her!

"Is this where you saw her?" she asked, sitting on the edge of the four-poster in Cassie's room. "Is she here now?"

"I saw her here and in the cellar, but like I told

you, I don't always see her. Sometimes I just hear her, or feel cold. She comes when she wants to. I don't see her now."

Jordan looked speculatively around the room. "Annie, come out, come out, wherever you are," she teased. "Do you think I'll be able to see her? I'm fourteen, too."

"Winona and I have the same birthday as Annie. Maybe that makes a difference. How do I know if you'll see her? Maybe she doesn't want you to see her."

"Why not?" Jordan asked. She bounced on the bed. "Was this her bed?"

"The four poster frame was, but Mom got a new mattress," said Cassie.

"Maybe she doesn't want you sleeping in it," Jordan said. "Maybe she really will howl all night."

"Jordie, just stop it. Don't try to scare me. It's hard enough already," said Cassie.

Jordan looked contrite. "I'm sorry. I get carried away. I've never been in on anything like this before. Let's go pick out a campsite." She looked impish. "Coming Annie?" she asked.

"If she's here, she can hear everything you say," said Cassie.

"I hope so," said Jordan.

They took their camp packs and walked out to the spring house and on to the graveyard, where Jordan studied each of the four graves. Cassie carefully read the inscriptions on the other three stones but she stayed away from Annie's grave.

John Charles Gwynne
Infant son of Joseph and Adele Gwynne
Taken to his Maker to the sorrow of his parents.
Born January 15, 1885
Died February 22, 1887
Age 2 yrs, 1 mo., 7 days

Adele Bowman Gwynne
Beloved wife of Joseph Gwynne
Mother of Annie and Johnnie
She was the light of our lives.
Born June 23, 1859
Died December 5, 1893

Joseph Gwynne
1854 - 1940

Sad, Cassie thought. No one had cared to inscribe anything more on Joseph's grave, a man who lived eighty-six years and died alone. His beautiful house couldn't have meant much to him any more, except for memories of his family. What was he like?

Her thoughts were interrupted by Jordan hollering from down the slope a ways. "Look, it's the perfect camping spot. Nice and flat, with a good view of the cemetery and the path coming up this way. No high brush for snakes to hide in." Jordan plopped down her sleeping bag and air mattress. "We don't even need a tent."

No tent? No way, thought Cassie. It felt too unprotected, not that a tent was going to be much protection. Too exposed. "You can sleep in the grass alone if you want to," she said. "I'm putting up the tent." She pulled the pop-up tent out of her pack and got started.

"Oh, all right," Jordan said. She joined in after all. It didn't take long to have their camp set up. "We can lie out here and tell ghost stories. I think there's even supposed to be a full moon tonight."

Cassie checked her watch. "We'll see if you still feel like telling ghost stories when it's really dark out here," she said. "Right now, we have to head back for supper. Mom brought a pot of chili to heat up."

She looked around, trying to memorize every feature of the area around the campsite. She couldn't believe they were going through with it. The closer evening came, the harder her heart was beating. Was Annie around? Campbell?

As they headed down the path, Cassie suddenly heard Annie's voice. "Is she your friend?" she asked. "Why did you bring her here?" Annie's icy hand took hers. "I thought you were MY friend," she said.

Cassie couldn't see her. All at once she realized that Annie had the advantage in this relationship. She could come and go as she pleased, be visible only when she wished to. She could cause no end of trouble for Cassie by appearing or talking to her when others were present.

Cassie stopped on the path. Annie tried to pull her back. Jordan turned to see Cassie apparently struggling with an invisible force, pulling her back up the path. She ran back to Cassie.

"Cassie?" she asked. "What's wrong?"

"Tell her to go away," said Annie. "I don't want her here." She gave Jordan a one-handed shove. Her hand went right through her.

Cassie gasped. "Annie's here," she said. "She's jealous."

"I am not jealous!" said Annie. "We have too much to do for you to spend time with her. Send her away."

"What's she saying, Cassie? What's she doing? I hear a whispering sound, but that's all." Jordan was all concern now.

"You can't see her?" Cassie asked Jordan.

"No, where is she?"

"I can't see her, either, but she is on my left side, holding my hand. She wants me to send you away. She says we -- she and I -- have too much work to do."

Jordan looked where she thought Annie would be. "Hello, Annie," she said. "My name is Jordan Dexter. I'm Cassie's friend. I'll help look for your letter, too. Don't you want another friend to help?"

For answer, Annie let just the faintest trace of her face appear. She let go of Cassie's hand and slipped right through Jordan, looking straight at Cassie as she did it. She whispered loudly, directly in Jordan's ear, "Cassie is MY friend, but since you're Felicity's granddaughter, you can stay if you help me." She fluttered on down the path toward the house, growing fainter until she disappeared.

"Did you see her?" Cassie whispered. "She was there for a moment, just her head. She's gone now, back to the house."

"No, but I think she tried to whisper in my ear," said Jordan. "I still couldn't hear what she said. I guess now we know that I'm not going to get to see Annie. Just my luck."

"Jordan, aren't you scared?" Cassie asked.

"Why? What's she going to do to me?" Jordan answered, but Cassie could see that her hands were shaking. She stuffed them into her jeans pockets.

Campout

nnie didn't appear again during supper. Afterward, Jordan insisted on exploring the attic.

"No way. Not tonight," Cassie protested. "I haven't been up there and I'm not going in the dark." She couldn't forget the face at the window, the hands around her neck, even if she was sure he wasn't in the house now. She didn't want to go anywhere connected with him.

"Oh, come on, Cassie," Jordan said. "There's no one here but your family and Annie. What's so scary about the attic? Besides, I told Annie I would help."

Cassie stared at Jordan, silent.

"Okay, already," said Jordan. "Not tonight. Tomorrow then. Let's go out to the tent and tell ghost stories. Maybe Annie will show up."

Cassie sighed. Jordan wasn't going to give up on seeing Annie, but Cassie was pretty sure it wasn't going to work, not for Jordan anyway.

As they gathered up their flashlights, water bottles and a camp lantern, Ben came rushing into the room dragging his sleeping bag.

"Can I camp out, too?" he asked.

Jordan gave Cassie a sideways glance. "N-o-o," she mouthed silently.

"Not this time, Ben," Cassie said. "This is my campout with Jordan. You can sleep out with me another time."

Ben stuck out his lower lip. His big eyes pleaded with Cassie. "Why can't I come?" he asked.

Just then Annie floated into view. All of her this time. "Take him," she demanded. "If you can take HER, you can take HIM," she said peevishly. "At least he belongs here. He's your brother. I wish I had MY brother to take camping!"

Cassie drew back as Annie planted her wraithlike form directly in front of her. Cold emanated from the ghost. Cassie felt as though someone had shoved her into a freezer. Annie stabbed in icy finger right through Cassie's shoulder. The pain was excruciating. Cassie shuddered. She couldn't talk to Annie in front of Ben, she just couldn't. She bit her lip.

"Oh, I see how it is," Annie said, a hint of bitterness in her voice. "You have a better friend to spend your time with now. Better than me. Better than your brother. We're not worth your time any more."

A jealous ghost! And she thought Annie was going to be friendly. Was this how it would be every time she brought a friend to Whispering Springs? She wouldn't dare.

"Grow up, Annie," she muttered under her breath.

"Come on, Jordan," she said, turning to leave the room. "I'm sorry, Ben. Not this time."

The path to the campsite was easy to follow in the moonlight. They could have done it even without flashlights. It was a perfect evening but Cassie kept looking around, expecting to hear someone in the brush or to see Annie skimming over the grass. She rubbed her shoulder where Annie's freezing finger had penetrated. It didn't really hurt anymore, but the memory wasn't easy to shake. Would Annie really harm her? Or Jordan? That would be stupid, she reasoned. If she did, Annie couldn't count on Cassie's help any longer.

"Annie," she whispered. "If you can hear me, please, please don't hurt anyone. Jordan and I are here to help." But she still didn't know how to help Annie or trap Jason Campbell.

Jordan was full of spooky stories. Cassie listened halfheartedly, but she was surprised to see that a faint Annie had settled herself on a stone near the tent. She seemed to be enthralled with Jordan's stories. Good, thought Cassie. Maybe she'll like Jordan after all.

When Jordan finally ran out of stories and began to fall asleep, Annie rose in the air over the tent and spread out like a thin mist through the clearing. The air was full of whispers, Annie talking on the wind.

"Listen, Cassie," said Jordan sleepily. "Do you hear the whispering?"

"Yes," said Cassie. "Annie is telling a real ghost story. Hers."

In the middle of the night, Cassie awoke. She thought she heard a rustling sound farther up the hill, just off the path. Annie? She looked out of the tent, but saw nothing in the moonlight. It must be my imagination, she told herself.

She lay awake for a long time, listening. Near dawn, just as she was falling asleep again, she heard the noise once more, this time much closer to the tent. There would be a soft crunch and then a pause, then another crunch, as though someone were trying to sneak up on them. She froze. Who, or what, was out there?

Suddenly a strong gust of wind tore through the trees as if a storm was coming. It was followed by a yelp of pain. Something fell and then went crashing away through the brush. Then there was silence again, except for the insect sounds.

Cassie could just make out Annie's whispers. She was no longer telling her stories. Now her voice came softly on the dawn breeze. "See, Cassie? I am your friend. He's gone now. I'm so tired . . . Beware. Beware." The whispers trailed off.

Cassie shook Jordan awake. "Something was out there. Someone," she corrected herself. "I think Annie scared him away. Let's head for the house. He might come back again."

Jordan rubbed her eyes sleepily. She hadn't heard a thing. "Hmmm?" she mumbled. She rolled over and went back to sleep.

Cassie shook her. "Come on, Jordan. I'm not

staying out here waiting for whoever it was to come back."

Jordan yawned and sat up. "I always miss the excitement," she said. She obediently picked up her flashlight and pillow and followed Cassie down the path. The sky was just beginning to turn pale in the east but it was still dark on the path. There was a hint of fog in the air.

Cassie and Jordan slipped quietly into the house and up the stairs to Cassie's room. They flopped on the four-poster, out of breath.

"You really didn't hear anything?" Cassie whispered.

"Not a thing. I was sound asleep." Jordan said.

"Someone, maybe Jason Campbell, was out there. What do you think he was going to do?"

"What could he do?" Jordan asked. "He can't very well do anything bad to you if he wants your help. I think you had a bad dream. Would that be so unusual after everything that's happened to you out here?"

While they were arguing about it, they heard Cassie's mother call, "Ben! Where's Ben?"

Everyone came running. Ben was gone.

It was Cassie who noticed that his sleeping bag was gone, too. Her heart sank. Did Ben go camping all alone? Was it his cry she heard in the night? She raced up the path toward their campsite. She had promised herself to protect her brother, but she thought he would be safe in the house with her parents. She never thought he would take his sleeping bag outdoors on his own!

"Ben!" she shouted. "Ben, where are you? Oh, God, please let Ben be all right!"

She almost missed him. He sat up in his sleeping bag, just off the path about twenty feet from their tent, partly hidden by a large rock.

"What's the matter, Cassie?" he asked sleepily.

"Oh, Ben, it's okay now," she said.

But it wasn't okay. It was bad enough that Ben wanted to go camping with her so much that he would sneak out here in the night and sleep by himself on the ground, just to be near her. But her heart nearly stopped beating when she realized that the sound she had heard, just before Annie scared someone away, was right here. Right where Ben was sleeping.

He was after Ben, she thought. She knew it as surely as if she had seen it. "Thank you, Annie. Thank you!" she said fervently.

As soon as Ben was safely back at the house and her mother understood what happened, Ben got a big hug and then a thorough scolding.

"Don't you EVER wander off without permission again!" their mother scolded him. "Especially not at night!"

"But Mom, I just went camping with Cassie," he protested.

"You didn't have permission to go with Cassie, and she didn't know you were there," his mother pointed out. "Go get cleaned up for breakfast while I think this over."

After a downcast Ben left the room Cassie said, "Mom, that man was out there last night. I heard him. I think he was after Ben."

"What makes you think it was some man and not an animal, or your imagination?" her mother asked. "Why would anyone be after Ben? Ben's fine!"

"Remember the sympathy cards?" Cassie asked. "Whoever it was, we're lucky something scared him away. Just watch him, that's all." She didn't dare say any more.

After breakfast, Jordan grabbed their flashlights and dragged Cassie to the stairs that led to the third story tower room and the attic. "I just KNOW there is something important up there," she said.

"You don't believe me, either, do you?" Cassie asked.

"Well, Cassie, I didn't hear or see anything last night," Jordan replied.

"But it happened!" Cassie insisted.

"Let's say it did," said Jordan. "What do you think that guy was going to do?"

"I don't know. Kidnap Ben, maybe?" There, she'd said it. The thought took her breath away.

Jordan frowned. "Why? It's not like your family is so rich or anything. He couldn't expect a big ransom."

"But what if we are rich, Jordan, and we just don't know it yet?" Cassie asked. "What if the treasure is real? If I don't find it for him, maybe he'd want to kidnap Ben, thinking my parents would turn the treasure over to him to get Ben back. And even if there isn't any treasure, he thinks there is!"

"Oh, my God, Cassie!" Jordan exclaimed. "You might be right. If that's possible, we HAVE to find the letter. Fast!"

Cassie felt cold brush past her, felt the goose bumps rising on her arms. Annie was with them, invisible. Watching us, Cassie thought. Listening. I don't want to be haunted.

"She's right," said Annie's disembodied voice. "I can't stop him forever. I'm not strong enough."

Kidnapped

Cassie took a deep breath. "Okay, let's go up to the tower room. We have to talk it over, just the three of us." She trudged up the stairs, watching Annie sail right through the door.

Jordan rushed into the small, octagonal-shaped room as soon as Cassie opened the door. She peered around as though she expected something startling and unusual to be there. The room was completely bare. The only things she seemed to find interesting were the smaller doors that opened off into the two wings of the attic. Jordan peeked through one into the gloom.

"Wait a minute," said Cassie. She sank to the floor and sat cross-legged. "I have to talk to Annie first."

A faint Annie floated over and settled down beside her.

"Annie, I found out who Miss Mossman's mother and grandmother were. Her grandmother was your Aunt Marie, and her mother was your cousin Dora."

Cassie could hear Annie let out a long sigh. "After all these years," she whispered. "Someone in my family. Someone related to me. No wonder she had the photo of my house and my letter. No wonder Mr. Campbell thinks she can help him." She turned to look directly into Cassie's eyes. "I have to see her," she said. "We have to stop him."

"But HOW?" Cassie asked. "I've tried and tried to think what to do, but even if we find the letter you want, he wants it, too. And today is the deadline."

"I don't know yet, but we'll find a way."

"I found this in Johnnie's toy chest," said Cassie, fishing the locket out of her pocket and opening it.

Annie touched it lovingly. "My mother saved it! It matches my iris brooch, doesn't it? Did you bring it, too?"

Cassie held out the brooch. "Did you ever think about what it says? I mean, could that be a clue, 'Treasure the Irises'?"

"I don't know," said Annie. "She always loved them. I never thought about it meaning anything else."

"Jordan?" Cassie called. Jordan had disappeared through the door into the west wing of the attic.

"In here," Jordan's voice was faint, coming from the far end of the house. "There's a little light from the window at the end. You have to be careful. There's only flooring in the middle."

Cassie switched on her flashlight and ducked under the door frame. She looked back to see whether Annie was coming. To her surprise, Annie didn't follow. She seemed to be listening intently to something Cassie couldn't hear and floated away through the window.

In the attic, Cassie could stand upright as long as she stayed near the center. There wasn't much there. Maybe it had been used for storage at one time, but everything must have been cleaned out, maybe moved to the cellar.

"It doesn't look like we'll find anything up here after all," she said, dejected. It wasn't so much that she thought they would, but she couldn't help hoping that Jordan might be right. Time was running out.

"You try the other side," said Jordan. "There must be a hundred places someone could hide a letter in an old house like this. You could stuff it just about anywhere. Even up here. In the rafters, maybe."

"And you could look forever and never find it," said Cassie. "If it's still there." But she couldn't give up, not yet.

She backed out and went to the other side of the attic. The door was stuck. She had to yank it open. It creaked eerily, the sound grating on her nerves like chalk on a blackboard.

The east side of the attic was a little lighter, with the morning sun coming in through a window at the far end. Once inside, she stood up and slowly walked the length of it. It was empty. She was almost back to the door, leaning down to go into the octagonal room, when she stepped on the edge of the flooring. The old board cracked. Cassie lost her balance but grabbed the door frame and landed on her knees, glad she was still on the flooring and hadn't gone crashing through the ceiling of the room below. Mom and Dad sure would have loved that! Another repair bill.

She examined the cracked board. No wonder it broke. It had a big knothole in it right at the edge. No one would use a board like that where it really counted. She pulled on it. She ought to show it to her dad. Maybe Jordan's teasing about crashing through the floors wasn't funny after all. Oh, stop it, she told herself. Dad said they had the house checked. It's just one little board in the attic.

She yanked one end of the board free and cried out in surprise. Tucked under the edge of the board, barely inside the attic door, was an envelope! With trembling hands she pulled it out. A hidden letter. Could this be it, at last?

Just as she turned it over and saw "Annie" penned in graceful script on the front, she heard her mother calling her from the front yard. She sounded desperate.

Cassie stuffed the envelope into her pocket and scrambled out of the attic. "Jordan," she yelled, "Something's wrong." She ran down the two flights of stairs and out into the yard. Jordan was close behind.

Her mother was crying out, "Ben, where are you, Ben?" She looked at Cassie with frightened eyes.

"Mom, what's wrong?" Cassie asked.

"Ben's gone. He was out here in the yard while your dad was painting the window frames. He was playing games in the bushes. You know, his imagination games, with a fort under those lilacs over there." She pointed. "The next thing we knew, he was gone. He doesn't answer when we call. He should know better than to wander off again!"

Cassie felt as though something were squeezing the breath out of her. She knew Ben hadn't wandered off. The thick lilac bushes were where she and Annie had seen Jason Campbell earlier that week. He had Ben! She was too late.

Cassie hugged her mother as tightly as she could. There was no use in keeping secrets now. She struggled to get control of herself, trying not to cry.

"That man I told you about -- he's dangerous. His name is Jason Campbell. I met him out here the day Kevin and Jordan took me rock hunting. He believes in the Gwynne treasure and he wants it. He sent me email that he was desperate and today was the deadline. He threatened Ben and Miss Mossman, and now he's kidnapped them. We have to find them before it's too late!" She remembered Campbell's message -- first Miss Mossman, then Ben. She was sure he had them both.

Cassie's mother held her out at arm's length and looked her directly in the eyes. "Cassie, this isn't your imagination, is it?" she asked. "How did you learn all this?"

"Mom, Annie has already protected me and Ben

from him more than once. She's been watching him and told me his name. You've got to believe me."

"Annie?" her mother asked. "Who is Annie?"

"Annie Gwynne, the girl who died here, the one whose father built this house."

"Oh, Cassie! Don't tell me any more stories about ghosts. This is no time for foolishness!"

"But she's HERE, Mom. Believe me."

Her mother closed her eyes and took a deep breath. She let it out slowly, her mouth tight with disapproval. "You and Jordan get out and look for your brother right now! I'll deal with you later. Dad's already gone up the path toward the spring. I'm calling the sheriff."

"Tell him about Jason Campbell, Mom," said Cassie. "He's real."

Where could they look, she and Jordan? Dad was already heading for the spring. She didn't know any other paths. If Ben had been in any of the usual places, they'd have found him. Maybe there would be a trail past the lilacs.

Cassie crawled under the tangle of lilac bushes. There were Ben's toy soldiers and his sheriff's star. Jordan crawled in beside her. She gave Cassie a hug.

It wasn't hard to see where someone could sneak away through the bushes as long as they crouched down. They'd still be well-hidden, especially from anyone at ground level. Jordan followed Cassie through the brush. About fifteen feet from Ben's fort, the path was still narrow but they could stand up.

"Sure you want to come?" Cassie asked. "If we do find him, it could be dangerous."

"I'm coming," said Jordan firmly. "I said I would help."

They walked for at least twenty minutes through brush and prairie meadows. They were far from anything familiar. Cassie didn't even know if they were still on Whispering Springs land. She began to wonder whether they would just go on and on across the prairie and never find anything, never find Ben. How much time were they wasting? She stopped on a small rise overlooking a creek in a deep ravine. What if they were lost?

She was amazed to see Annie, dim and hazy, below them near the water. She looked up at Cassie and put her fingers to her lips.

"Why?" Cassie mouthed silently.

Annie pointed farther down the path, at the side of a small hill above the ravine.

At first, Cassie didn't understand. She couldn't see anything unusual ahead. She climbed down toward Annie, ducking low, keeping quiet. Then she saw it. A dugout. There was a door in the hillside. Beyond it, half-hidden in a clump of brush was a battered pickup truck. Jason Campbell's hideout? She looked at Annie, who nodded. Cassie pointed back along the path the way they came. "Let's meet back there," she whispered.

The three of them found a place behind some bushes where they wouldn't easily be seen.

"He has Ben," said Annie. "I heard something from the tower room, so I went out. I followed them. He has a gun."

"Jordan, go back and get help. Tell them where to come," Cassie said.

"But Cassie, you can't stay here alone. It's too dangerous. What are you going to do?" Jordan asked.

"I'm not alone. Annie is with me," Cassie said. "Campbell can't hurt her."

"But he can hurt you. And Ben," said Jordan.

"I know," said Cassie, "but someone has to watch and see what happens. What if he gets away? What if he hurts them or takes them somewhere?"

"Okay, Cassie. Just be safe, all right?" said Jordan. She started back along the path.

"Annie, we have to find some way to catch him," Cassie said. She was desperate. How could two girls, one a ghost, deal with a man like Campbell? Out of habit, she felt in her pocket for her lucky stone. Her hand closed on the crumpled letter. She pulled it out. Please, please, she prayed soundlessly, let Annie really be my friend now.

"Annie, I found this in the attic just as you left and I heard my mother calling for Ben. It might be your letter."

Annie ran her hands gently over the envelope but did not attempt to take it. She faced Cassie, tears welling in her eyes. She took Cassie's hands, lightly, softly. Annie's hands were still icy cold, but Cassie felt affection in them.

"Use it to lure him out," she said. "Go up on the hill above the dugout and tell him you have it, that you will give it to him if he lets them go."

"But what if he just comes after me with the gun and takes it?" asked Cassie.

"I won't let him," said Annie. "Stay down where he can't see you so he won't have a chance to aim."

The two girls looked hard at each other. It was a terrible risk.

"You don't think we should wait for Jordan to bring help?" asked Cassie.

"No. He's planning something," said Annie. "I don't know what it is, but we can't wait."

Cassie took a deep breath. She put the letter back into her pocket.

"No matter what happens, thank you Annie," she said. She started up over the hill, keeping herself low and out of sight.

Rescue

When Annie signaled that Cassie was directly above the dugout, Cassie shouted, "Mr. Campbell. I found the letter. My parents don't know about it yet. You can have it, but you have to let Ben and Miss Mossman go free first."

Nothing happened. He didn't answer. Maybe Annie was wrong. Maybe he wasn't in there, or maybe that wasn't where he was keeping them.

She picked up a rock and threw it down the hill, hoping it would make some noise near the door. She could hear it bounce down the ravine. Still nothing.

She looked around for Annie, but Annie was nowhere to be seen. Had she deserted her after all, leaving her for Jason Campbell to come after with his gun? She lay flat on her stomach in the long grass, tense and still. What would she do now if Annie was gone and he came for the letter? She didn't believe he would just take it from her and walk away. Not if she could identify him.

"Mr. Campbell," she yelled. "You'll never find the treasure without the letter."

Still no answer. Maybe she should give up and hide, wait for Jordan to bring help. But what if no one believed Jordan, either, and no one came? Or just her dad, who refused to believe Campbell was dangerous?

"Ben," she hollered. "Are you there?"

There was a faint rustling sound. Someone was in the grass approaching her! Campbell was no fool. He had come up the hill the long way and circled around behind her, hoping to catch her unaware. She realized the new danger now. Once he saw her and had the gun pointed at her, she would be the next captive. There would be no struggle over the letter, no saving anyone.

He was behind her but hadn't seen her yet. Cassie inched herself forward. There was a place where the hillside dropped off sharply into the deep ravine, a small cliff. She hoped fervently that Annie was there somewhere and understood what she was doing.

Near the edge of the ravine, still flat on the ground, she called, "Mr. Campbell, where are you? I'll give you the letter, but you have to let my brother go first."

He was almost on top of her!

"Fat chance, you little brat!" he growled. He stuffed the gun into his waistband and reached down to grab her.

Before he had a chance to get his hands on her, Annie charged him from behind with incredible speed. This was no faint vision. Cassie had never seen Annie so clearly. Her expression was fierce and determined as she held out her hands in front of her like two battering rams. They caught Campbell squarely in the back and sent him flying over the edge of the ravine. He landed with a dull thud on a gravel area next to the creek. He lay still, knocked out, one leg bent at an odd angle. Broken, Cassie realized. She gasped.

What now? Where was Annie? There was no trace of her.

Cassie scrambled down the side of the hill and along the path to the dugout. Campbell had left the door unlocked. She pushed it open warily, expecting it to be dark in the dugout, but there was a camp lantern burning. Hesitantly she took a step inside. What if he had an accomplice?

"Oh, Ben! Miss Mossman!" she exclaimed. They were duct-taped to two old chairs, with gags in their mouths. She ran to them, fishing in her pocket for her knife to cut them free. They made frantic sounds behind the gags.

Before she could start, Annie's faint, faceless voice warned her, "Tie him up first. What if he comes to?"

"Annie, where are you?" she asked.

"Tired. Can't make myself visible," was the hushed reply. "Later." Her voice trailed off to nothing.

Cassie looked around the dugout for something

she could use to tie Campbell up. There was a roll of duct tape on a makeshift table. She ran out the door with it and wrapped layers of it round and round his hands and feet. Then she ran tape between his hands and feet and put a strip across his mouth. When she was sure there was no way he could get free, she ran back into the dugout to cut her brother and neighbor loose.

Duct tape still hanging from their clothing, wrists and ankles, Ben and Miss Mossman hugged Cassie. She held them tight, not wanting to let them go, holding back tears of relief.

"He is a very bad man," Ben said. "He said he wanted to play with me and he had a real fort to show me. I didn't want to go with him, but he tied me up and stuffed that thing in my mouth and carried me away. Why, Cassie? Why did he do that?"

"You're right, Ben. He is a bad man. He thinks there is a treasure somewhere at Whispering Springs. He thought he could get it if he kidnapped the two of you for ransom, I guess. Are you all right?"

"Yes, we're all right," answered Miss Mossman, though she looked pale and shaken. "But I don't know what would have happened if you hadn't come along just then. He was threatening to shoot one of us to prove to everyone that he was serious. He said he had a cell phone and could call your parents to make them turn over the treasure if they wanted us back. He wouldn't listen to us that no one knew about any treasure. How did you find us?"

"Annie," Cassie said. "She followed him when he took Ben. She's the one who pushed him over the edge of the ravine."

"Annie?" Miss Mossman looked at Cassie questioningly. "The girl who died so long ago? But how could she?"

"She's still here. She's a ghost."

Miss Mossman smiled slowly. "It was her voice then," she said.

Ben's eyes grew wide. He peered around, looking for Annie. "A REAL ghost?" he asked. "A ghost you can SEE?"

Cassie nodded.

"Is she the one who whispers?"

Cassie nodded again.

"We heard her," he said. "She talked to us. I wasn't scared. Is she here now?"

"I don't think so, Ben. It's hard for her to do something like pushing a big man over a cliff. I think she floats away and rests. Did you really hear her voice?"

"It was a girl's voice, but no one was there," said Ben.

How could it be, after all these years, when her own father couldn't hear her? Cassie marveled. Annie must have put all her strength into helping them. Her own little brother was dead, but she could help save Cassie's.

They followed Cassie outside, pulling off pieces of duct tape. Campbell's gun had fallen out of his waistband as he tumbled down the ravine. Cassie picked it up. She knew nothing about guns. Didn't know if it was loaded or if the safety was on, but she knew she didn't want it anywhere near him. Or Ben. She took it into the dugout and put it on the table, went back outside and shut the door.

"You said he had a cell phone. Do you know where it is?"

"In the pocket of his jacket," said Ben.

Cassie warily approached the unconscious man. Even trussed up in duct tape he might figure out some way to hurt her if he came to. It was the first time she got a good look at him. She had expected him to look evil, ugly even, but he didn't. He was so ordinary-looking. She wondered how badly hurt he was, whether he would die.

"Which pocket?" she asked. She didn't want to go poking around looking for it. It was all she could do to force herself to be that close to him.

"I think he had it in the right one," Miss Mossman said. "He's right handed."

That was lucky, since the left one was under him. Cassie carefully slid her hand into the pocket and drew out the phone. Then she retreated to the front of the dugout and called her mother's cell phone. There was no answer! Wouldn't her mother carry the phone in an emergency like this? Frantically, she tried to remember the new number for the phones at Whispering Springs but she couldn't.

911. She punched in the numbers. She didn't

wait for the dispatcher to say anything. As soon as the call was answered, she said, "Please send help now! A man named Jason Campbell kidnapped my little brother and my neighbor. We tricked him and he fell. He's unconscious and I tied him up with duct tape and took his gun."

"Where are you? Can you give me your name and location?"

"I don't know where we are. About a twenty minute hike from the Old Cranston Place on Mill Creek, near Alma. I think we went mostly south-west, but I can't be sure. My name is Cassie Wade. Please, my parents are somewhere there looking for us. I can't get them on my mother's cell phone." She gave them directions to Whispering Springs and her mother's number.

The First Letter

No one felt like eating supper. They were still at Whispering Springs, telling and retelling each person's story of what happened that afternoon after Cassie's mother discovered Ben was missing. The sheriff was there taking statements. Campbell was safely in custody and had been taken to a hospital. The sheriff told them he was a wanted criminal, living and working in Topeka under a false name. Apparently he had huge gambling debts and if he didn't pay them by the next day, the people he owed had threatened to kill him. He was desperate for money to pay them off and save his life.

"What I don't understand is why he thought he could get what he wanted from Cassie," her father said. "I don't see how he expected her to find the treasure if he couldn't."

"He's not talking much, but from what we were able to put together, he started looking for the treasure a couple of weeks before you bought the place," said the sheriff. "It was just his bad luck that the property sold when it did. He'd heard some rumors about the treasure, and was desperate enough to hope he'd find it and pay off his debts. He'd been doing odd jobs with a company that does home repairs and using the opportunities to look for good places to rob.

"Apparently, he thought he'd struck gold, so to speak, when he found that letter and photo at Miss Mossman's house. It convinced him that he was on the right track, that the treasure really did exist. He knew then that there was a hidden letter that could help him find it, but with your family coming out to work on the house, he didn't dare get in there as often to search for it. He couldn't take the chance on being discovered. He got the idea to frighten Cassie into finding it for him."

"But what if she never did? What was he going to do then?" asked her mother.

"Campbell believed that you and your husband, and probably Miss Mossman, all knew about the treasure. As he put it, why else would you have bought the run-down old house? He was half certain you already had the letter and Cassie would just have to find it in your things. He hoped to make off with the treasure quietly, assuming you hadn't removed it yet. But if Cassie failed him, he thought he could force Miss Mossman to tell him where it was, or make you come up with it somehow by kidnapping your son. He apparently thought the kidnapping would make you turn it over if you had found it."

"That doesn't make any sense," said Cassie's

dad. "None of us knew where the treasure or the letter was. We didn't even believe they existed."

"You're right, but Campbell didn't know that. I think his judgement was clouded by fear, for one thing. The people to whom he owed money aren't merciful. And for another, he just couldn't believe he'd lost his chance at a fortune he could have taken from a deserted house just because someone decided to buy it after all these years. He was sure that you must be interested in the house for the same reason he was. You're all tremendously lucky it turned out all right. Campbell may not be terribly bright, but he is a dangerous man."

"Cassie, why in the world didn't you tell us about the threatening email from Campbell?" her father demanded.

"Dad, I tried and tried to tell you about him," Cassie said. "You never would listen to me. By the time he sent the email and told me terrible things would happen to Ben if I told anyone, I believed him, and I didn't think you'd believe me."

"It's a typical ploy of criminals, Mr. Wade," said the sheriff, "particularly when dealing with children. They threaten to do terrible things if the victim tells anyone and it scares them into silence."

"I wish we had listened to you, Cassie," her father said. "I just couldn't imagine anyone dangerous out here on a deserted old farm. And you were telling me all those crazy ghost stories at the same time. How was I to know?" He put his head in his hands.

"Thank God you're all safe!"

Ben told his story over and over. He wanted to be sure his mom knew he hadn't just wandered off.

"I believe you, Ben," she kept saying, hugging him to her.

No one mentioned Annie. Jordan kept looking at Cassie, who would shake her head. What good would it do to bring her up now? They'd think she was crazy. Just listen to her dad.

Miss Mossman seemed to have come through the ordeal fine. She was entranced with the house and its history, fascinated that once her great-aunt and cousins had lived here. When things finally began to calm down a bit, she called everyone to the living room and announced that she had found the photo of the house, minus the frame, and the letter for Annie in the dugout. She pulled them from the pocket of her smock.

"Let's read it!" Jordan begged.

"Not without Annie," said Miss Mossman.

Cassie saw the look that passed between her parents. She could almost hear them thinking. Annie again. What kind of nonsense is this?

"What do you mean, not without Annie?" Cassie's father demanded. "She's been dead over a hundred years!"

"Dead, but not gone," said Miss Mossman. "This afternoon, when Ben and I were in the dugout with Mr. Campbell, we had just about lost all hope of being found alive. He was threatening to shoot us. We were terrified. Then a soft voice whispered to us. 'I'll help you,' it said. 'Be brave and wait.' Ben heard it, too. We didn't know who or what it was until after Cassie and Annie rescued us. Cassie told us about Annie and what she did to save us. I know she is here somewhere, waiting, just like she has been waiting all these years for the letters from her mother."

They really heard her! And they believed, Cassie thought. Was it because they believed? Annie had finally managed to make someone else realize she was there. Cassie was inexpressibly glad. She put her hand into her pocket to touch the iris brooch. Maybe it would bring Annie to them. But her hand found the other letter. In all the panic and excitement, she had forgotten about it. Should she bring it out now? She decided to wait until Miss Mossman had read the one she found.

"You can't be serious! What in tarnation is it about this place?" Cassie's father exploded. "It's bad enough that we've gone through this ordeal with Campbell without this nonsense about ghosts coming up again. I've been hearing about ghosts and werewolves for weeks. Don't tell me you think Annie is real, too."

Miss Mossman seemed unperturbed by his outburst. "There are many things in this world that don't fit tidy explanations, Daniel," she said. "I'm not asking you to believe me. I just want to invite Annie to be with us when I read the letter. It is addressed to her, after all, and Ben and I probably wouldn't be here with you if she hadn't saved us. We all owe her a huge debt of thanks."

Cassie's mother put her arm around Miss Mossman's shoulders. "If you think it's the right thing to do, we will invite her." Her tone was loving and friendly, but she clearly thought she was just humoring her old neighbor.

Miss Mossman waited until everyone was settled. Then she began, "Annie, some of us here owe our lives to you. Some of us don't believe you exist, but I invite you to be with us while I read the letter your mother sent to my grandmother so long ago."

She held the photo and the letter up for all to see. Cassie handed Miss Mossman her pocket knife and she slit open the envelope.

Dear Annie,

I must write quickly so that our friend Victoria can take this to the post. I will not be with you much longer. The doctor can't do anything for me. I am sad to leave you motherless for I love you with all my heart. I hope you grow up well and happy and have a good life but there is a family secret you must deal with when you are older. I wrote everything down in a letter hidden here. I cannot tell you where for fear your father might find it and destroy it. Your Aunt Marie will keep this letter for you until you are of age.

Remember The Foot Trail Under C.

Keep me always in your heart,

Your Loving Mother

The room was hushed. Whether they believed in Annie's ghost or not, they were curious about the letter from a dying mother about the Gwynne family secret. But what was that nonsense about a foot trail? Was Annie's mother delirious? Cassie wondered what everyone was thinking, especially Annie. Cassie looked around, hoping to see her. Surely she wouldn't miss this, even if she were terribly tired. There was no sign of her.

No one said anything for a long time. Jordan seemed lost in thought.

"It's an anagram," said Jordan, breaking the silence.

"What's an anagram?" asked Cassie.

"That thing about the foot trail. If you rearrange the letters, it says 'under the attic floor.'"

"That's where I found the letter!" exclaimed Cassie.

"Oh, for heaven's sake!" said Cassie's father. "This is ridiculous!"

Cassie watched, fascinated, as a soft, hazy version of Annie's face appeared right in front of her father.

"No it's not. My mother and I used to play word games a lot," said Annie. "I hope I would have figured it out, if I had lived, but Cassie already found the letter."

"Annie," Cassie whispered. "You are listening."

Annie's face had disappeared, but Cassie felt the barest touch of a soft, cold hand. She breathed a sigh of relief. Annie would hear her letter at last. She pulled it from her jeans pocket. It was badly crumpled.

"What's that now?" her mother asked.

"It's the other letter, the one that was hidden here," Cassie answered. "I found it in the attic this afternoon, just when you called out that Ben was missing."

She opened it. In the envelope along with the letter were a rosary and a badly bent photo of Annie's parents, their wedding photo. Joseph and Adele looking young and happy. Cassie stared.

"Look, Annie, can you see it?" she cried. "I'm sorry it got bent in my pocket." She held it out.

For just an instant, invisible hands supported the photo in the air and then it fell. Cassie caught it. There was an audible gasp from Cassie's mother.

"Cool!" said Jordan.

Cassie began to read.

The Secret

My Dearest Annie,
November 30, 1893

As I write this letter, I am dying. It grieves me that I will leave you motherless and never share your future as you grow into a woman. My only consolation is that you are, at only ten years of age, already a fine person. I will look upon you from the hereafter and find joy in seeing your life unfold.

There are things worse than death, Annie. I am writing this letter not only to say goodbye and to tell you how much I love you, but to tell you something important about our family. You are too young to be burdened with it now, but the day will come when our terrible family secret will be yours to deal with.

When I met and married your father, he was a wealthy young man with a ranch that was growing more and more successful. He was charming, handsome, and very devoted to me. He has been a good and loving husband. He loves you, and loved Johnnie, more than his life.

But Joseph is a flawed man. He suffers from a deadly sin. He knows it, and it causes him great anguish, but even his faith has not helped him to fight it. Your father is filled with Greed.

I never asked Joseph about money. He provided for us generously. He was secretive, but nothing seemed amiss. It was when Johnnie died that I found out his awful secret. He was inconsolable and kept saying he lost his only son as punishment for his sins. I couldn't understand how he could think he had anything to do with our baby's death.

One night, about two weeks after Johnnie was buried, Joseph was so grief-stricken he got terribly drunk and finally confided in me about how he had gotten rich.

As a young man, he had Gold Fever. There were rumors of gold in the Black Hills, land that was set aside for the Indians by treaty. No white men were supposed to go there. Some sneaked in anyway, especially after Custer took an expedition there in 1874 and found gold.

Your father and his best friend, John Sellars, were two of those men who broke the treaty and headed into the Black Hills to look for placer gold. They were lucky. They weren't found and evicted and they evaded the Indians. Few of the miners who went in to pan for gold found much. Most of the mining in the Hills required special equipment and large companies to get it out, but Joseph and John struck it rich on their own.

That was when their troubles started. They got into arguments over whether to take what they had panned and leave or stay and try to find more. They argued about how to divide up the gold and what stories to tell their families and friends about how they got it. One day they both got drunk and started swinging punches. It probably wouldn't have ended in anything serious except that John picked up a big tree branch and came after Joseph. Instead of just getting out of the way, Joseph threw an ax at John. He never intended to cause him harm, but he had killed his best friend.

Joseph feared he might be in trouble with the law for being on Sioux land and he didn't know whether anyone would believe his self-defense story. An ax against a tree branch didn't sound good. He buried John, then took all the gold and ran. He went to Colorado and lived there for a couple of years before coming back to Kansas a rich man.

He told John's parents their son died in a mining accident and was buried in South Dakota. They believed him. He bought this land and built this house, but he never told anyone about his past, though it tortured him every day of his life. He named our baby after his dead friend. From the day John Sellars died, Joseph was always afraid he would someday have to pay the price. He convinced himself that the price was our son's death. After Johnnie died, he couldn't stand to have anything in the house that reminded him of our baby boy.

I urged him to try to make amends, but how? He was still in the grip of gold. We could easily have lived well on the profit from the ranch by this time, but he could not give up his gold. Gold Fever seems to be incurable. I could not convince him that he would be happier if he gave the gold away, whether to John's family or to the Sioux (to whom it most rightly belongs) or to the Church.

Now I am dying and Joseph is torturing himself with thoughts that his sins have brought this upon us, too. It will not be easy to live with him after my death. I wish you well, my little daughter. Be strong.

I tried to persuade your father to tell you our family's secret when you come of age, but he insists that he will never taint you with his sins. I asked him to give you a letter from me and he refused, so I asked Victoria to hide *this where he will never find it.*

I hope that when you grow older, you will decipher the clue I gave you on your tenth birthday. If you are as clever as I think you are, you will find this letter and your father's gold. If not, you will be no worse off than your father would have wished. I cannot tell you plainly in case someone else finds this letter. Maybe you will be wiser than either of your parents about how to make peace with the world.

Your Loving Mother

For several long minutes there was complete silence in the room. Cassie pulled the iris brooch out of her pocket and examined it again. The clue WAS there. "Treasure the Irises."

"It's real," whispered Annie. "The treasure is real. My poor father. No wonder he was unhappy. He killed his best friend. He kept his fortune and lost everyone he loved. I hope he's at peace now." She began to take a filmy form, one hand on her mother's letter.

"I'm sure he is, Annie," said Miss Mossman.

Had anyone else heard her? Could they see her? Cassie looked around the room. Her mother and Jordan seemed petrified, like stone people with wide eyes, staring at the spot where Annie was slowly taking shape. They're beginning to believe, Cassie thought, and now they can see her.

It was true. Annie was visible, but not to all of them.

"I don't know what kind of apparition you think you're seeing, but you're letting your imaginations get the better of you," her father said. "What's to be gained from this? Let's figure out where that treasure is!"

"Hush, Daniel," her mother said. To Annie she said, "What a heartbreaking story. Thank you for saving my children. Your mother would be very proud of you."

Annie smiled at her. She floated over to her and took her hand. Cassie saw her mother flinch at the cold, but she did not draw away.

Cassie kept turning the brooch over and over. The clue was there. The letter said it was. "But the irises. I don't understand the clue," she said.

"There are irises carved all around the front door," said Jordan.

Annie floated over to the door frame. Cassie followed. What would some irises on a door frame have to do with a hidden treasure? She almost said so, almost asked her father if she could dig up the iris beds around the house, when she saw it -- in the graceful carving was an exact copy of the brooch she was holding in her hand.

"Look, Annie," she said. "It matches." She held

the brooch up beside the wood design. When she looked at it closely, it seemed that part of the carving had a tiny line around it, as though it were separate in some way. She pressed it.

They heard the click, as though a latch had been lifted. The entire carved panel swung outward. Inside was a tall, narrow cabinet, built into the thick stone wall. It was filled with a stack of small canvas bags, each marked with a number; 5, 10 or 20. Cassie put out a trembling hand. Was this it, in those bags?

Her father lifted the top one off the pile and set it on the floor. He opened the tie around the top and caught his breath.

"Gold," he whispered. "If all those bags are full of gold, there is an incredible fortune here."

Annie stared at the sacks of gold coins in wonder. The stories were true!

Treasure

Cassie's father sat down heavily. He was speechless. In his hands he held thousands of dollars' worth of precious $20.00 gold pieces from the late 1870s and 1880s.

For a long moment, no one spoke. Then everyone crowded around and started talking at once. They marveled at the glittering coins.

Ben danced around the room with a gold piece in his hands singing, "We're rich, we're rich."

"But are we?" asked Cassie. "Is it really finders keepers? Whose gold is it?"

"Honey, we bought the property and everything on it," her father said.

"But if you buy stolen property, you don't get to keep it, do you?" Cassie persisted. Much as she wished all that money were theirs, she couldn't forget Adele's letter so easily.

"How is this stolen property?" her father asked. "It's U.S. coinage. It belonged to Gwynne. We came by it honestly."

"But he didn't," said Annie.

"It would have been Annie's, if she had lived. I

think she should have some say in what happens to her inheritance," said Miss Mossman.

"What kind of fool do you take me for?" asked Cassie's father. "You want to let a ghost -- that is, if I thought there were such a thing -- tell us what to do with a fortune in gold coins? There's more money here than I could make in a lifetime!"

"I think we should find out what she has to say, Daniel," said his wife.

"You, too? I don't believe this!" he exclaimed.

"Daniel, I didn't accept the existence of Annie's ghost, either, until this evening. Open your eyes. She saved your children. She's here beside you. You heard her mother's letter."

"That was in 1893, for heaven's sake! What does that have to do with our finding the gold today?"

"Daddy, do you have Gold Fever?" asked Ben.

His father glared at him.

"Ben, clearly you do not have any idea what this represents."

"Yes I do, Daddy. If we keep it, we can buy anything we want."

Their dad turned to the sheriff. "What's your opinion?" he asked.

The officer shrugged. "A couple of good lawyers might be able to make a case either way, but who's going to try to take it from you? There aren't any living legal heirs with any current property rights."

Annie stood off to the side, looking dazed and

uncertain. Cassie went to her. She hesitated for only a moment before putting her arms around her ghostly friend. She expected the cold. What she hadn't expected was that her hands, her arms, went right through the filmy girl. Annie had no substance at all. But Cassie stayed, stayed connected to Annie. I can give her my warmth, she thought. At least I can give her that.

"I thought when I found my mother's letter, everything would be all right," said Annie. "I'd be happy. I'd know the secret and could leave at last. I never thought I'd find out something so sad or that the treasure would be a burden. I can't be at peace now that my mother has left me to decide how to deal with it. Not until it's over."

"What do you think is the right thing to do, Annie?" Miss Mossman asked. Cassie's father started to protest, but she held up her hand. "Wait, Daniel. Let's hear what she has to say."

"It's not rightly ours. Not any of us," said Annie. "But if Cassie hadn't found it, it would still be locked away, maybe forever, or until someone tore down the house. It wouldn't be doing anyone any good. So, what I think would be fair . . . well, if it were my decision to make, I would give half of it back to the Indians. I don't know how you do that, but there must be some way to give it to a Sioux organization. And the other half, part of that should be set aside for Cassie and Ben, for their future. And some should go to Winona."

She turned to Cassie's father. "The rest you can keep."

"Daddy, you should listen to Annie," said Ben. "There's enough for everyone to share. We're supposed to share, right?"

Their father pursed his lips and frowned but he agreed to listen to Annie's proposal. Cassie and Miss Mossman explained it to him. He drew a long, deep breath and let it out slowly, looked down at the coins in his hand. He hadn't heard Annie, but plainly the proposal had come from somewhere. Not from anyone he could see in this room. He was obviously uncomfortable with that idea. He glanced around the room nervously.

"That sounds fair," he said at last. "I understand Joseph Gwynne better than you think. It's not easy to give up all that money. I'll go along with it if it's the only way to get the ghost out of my family. But only if you all agree."

"Thank you, Daddy," Cassie exclaimed. She threw her arms around him.

"We should be thanking Annie," said her mother. "She not only saved our children and our friend, but I think her solution is the best one."

"I hope you'll still thank me when you realize what we are giving up," he said.

"Before you do anything else with it, you'd better get it into a bank vault," said the sheriff. "If word of this gets out, Jason Campbell might be the least of your worries. I'll arrange for secure transportation."

"Cassie," said Annie. "Can you do that for me? Make sure that half the gold goes to the Sioux? Maybe then our family will rest in peace. It's worth lots more now than when he took it, isn't it?"

"Don't worry, Annie. We'll do it," Cassie answered.

"I'm so tired," said Annie. Her voice was growing softer. "Let's go up to my room. Bring the pictures and the letters." Her ethereal form, wispy and light, drifted toward the stairs. "I want to hear them one more time."

Upstairs, Cassie propped the photos on the walnut desk. She put the locket and the iris brooch beside them. Annie hovered there, memorizing the pictures, remembering her mother. As the evening stars came out, Cassie read the letters to Annie again. When she read the last words, "Maybe you will be wiser than either of your parents about how to make peace with the world. Your Loving Mother," Annie slowly drifted out the open window toward the sky.

"Goodbye, Cassie, my friend," came the last murmur on the evening breeze.

The End

Jerri began writing stories with her spelling words in the second grade. As soon as she learned to read, she started getting in trouble at school for reading when she should have been working on assignments. She has loved to read and write ever since.

Jerri grew up in Manhattan, Kansas and returned there in 1992 after living in Germany, Japan, Hawaii, Puerto Rico, Illinois, Kentucky and Virginia with her husband Peter, a career Army attorney who now teaches German in the middle schools. They have two grown sons and three grandchildren.

Jerri's other books are:

Izzie - Growing Up on the Plains in the 1880s
Imagicat
Johnny Kaw - The Pioneer Spirit of Kansas
Kansas Katie - A Sunflower Tale

Write to Jerri at: Send email to:
Jerri Garretson   RavenstonePress@netscape.net
Ravenstone Press
P.O. Box 1791
Manhattan KS 66505-1791

What does a man gain by winning the whole world
at the cost of his true self?
Mark 8:36

With Heartfelt Thanks To:

My dear friends
who read and critiqued the manuscript:

My virtual sister
Alice McLerran

Shelly Larkins
Dr. Therese Bissen Bard

My husband
Peter W. Garretson

Many thanks to
Robert and Carolyn Miller
for permission to use a modified photograph
of their beautiful home in Beloit, Kansas
on the cover.
It was built in 1880
with native stone from the
Manhattan, Kansas area.